Twice Chosen

Neill Nutter

CROSSBOOKS

CrossBooks™
1663 Liberty Drive
Bloomington, IN 47403
www.crossbooks.com
Phone: 1-866-879-0502

©*2010 Neill Nutter. All rights reserved.*

No part of this book may be reproduced, stored in a retrieval system, or transmitted by any means without the written permission of the author.

First published by CrossBooks 1/21/2010

ISBN: 978-1-6150-7097-8 (sc)

Library of Congress Control Number: 2009943348

Printed in the United States of America
Bloomington, Indiana

This book is printed on acid-free paper.

Prologue

It was early morning, and the shadows in the narrow alley were long and cold. Looking out a window of one of the tenements that lined the alley, a figure could be seen, moving stealthily, as if searching for something or someone.

He looked both old and ageless, yet non-descript, and that was exactly what he desired – to move and mingle without drawing attention. His face at first impression showed unusual beauty: the shape of the nose, the cut of the chin, and deep, black piercing eyes. But a closer look revealed a hideousness that defied description. Those eyes were dark with arrogance and hatred, windows to a world that caused the soul to wither and die.

These cheerless alleys often yielded useful pickings, clues to the lives of those that lived nearby and information that could be used to manipulate, for he had a cruel agenda. His scheme was to trap the foolish or unwary into doing his bidding.

As he prowled about the alley, he heard a sound from somewhere nearby. It was a cry of distress and misery, yet the alley was empty – no animals, no people – just the litter blown in by the wind or abandoned by indifference. He looked intently for the source.

The sound came from a cardboard carton lying near garbage cans carelessly filled with the flotsam and jetsam of the lives dwelling nearby. He went to the box, carefully lifting the flaps, not knowing what might be found.

At the bottom of the carton was a baby, a newborn little boy lying in a pool of afterbirth, as if the birth had occurred in the box. Looking past the gory mess, he knew this newborn was a healthy child, at least for now. As light entered the space, the cries of hunger and discomfort intensified.

The figure straightened and rubbed his jaw in thought. "Should I leave the baby and continue?"

"Life," and he contemptuously spat the word out, "means nothing to me. . . . , unless to be used."

As he considered the possibilities, he selfishly decided that this tiny, messy human might prove to be most valuable to him. Didn't he have many that were already his, those who owed him their very souls for favors done? He chuckled evilly, closed the box, lifted it carefully, and disappeared into the shadows.

An intangible group of perhaps a dozen was meeting in a dimension no living individual on this earth had ever seen. It seemed a transition from something to nothing, or perhaps the opposite. It resembled gloom or darkness but not as humans see gloom or darkness, for this was a gathering of beings, faceless and formless, yet projecting an aura that confirmed their existence or presence.

They were planning what they believed would place themselves beyond all others and achieve, for eternity, the right to control all. One being was clearly the Dominant.

"I found an abandoned soul today that we can shape into the one that will enable us to dominate once and for all. We have been thwarted in our quest long enough. This time we will win - forever."

Contents

Chapter 1	The Commission	1
Chapter 2	Love Takes Root	7
Chapter 3	Preparing for Education	15
Chapter 4	Leily Borhan	27
Chapter 5	Weekends and Breaks	37
Chapter 6	A Change in the Wind	43
Chapter 7	The Hajj	51
Chapter 8	Conclusions	61
Chapter 9	Try Again	67
Chapter 10	Plans and Intentions	79
Chapter 11	Tibet	87
Chapter 12	Surprise!	95
Chapter 13	What Now?	109
Chapter 14	Real Enlightenment	123
Chapter 15	A Long Journey	133
Chapter 16	Home At Last	143
Chapter 17	Making the Break	149
Chapter 18	A Glorious Encounter	157
Chapter 19	A New Day!	159

Chapter 1

The Commission

The large car moved quickly down the boulevard. The median was landscaped and marked by stately trees. Stonewalls and wrought iron fences marked the perimeter of the boulevard only to be interrupted by gates or gatehouses. It was obviously a very affluent area, with only an occasional glimpse of imposing homes set like islands amidst a sea of hedges and manicured lawns and gardens.

The big car turned from the street at an especially impressive gate. Engraved on a block embedded in one of the gateposts was 'The Planes,' a name given to the many sycamore trees planted along the drive and numerous on the estate. The driver stopped by a dark brown cast iron cabinet that was built into the stone gatepost. The driver's window went down, and he reached across to the box, opened the door and picked up a phone. He quickly dialed four digits, spoke a few words, and the gates quietly opened. As the car cleared the gate area, the gates quickly shut with an authoritative thump.

The car moved rapidly down a drive surrounded by formal gardens and great trees, toward a magnificent building that was like a large English country house. The mansion was built of cut stone, which seemed to be granite, and had a slate roof. On the one hand it was very large with a number of levels sprawling in several directions, but everything was of such a massive scale the building did not appear imposing. That it had been built many years before was obvious for many of the walls were nearly covered by ivy. There were at least a dozen or more chimneys, and the windows were made of many small panes leaded into iron frames.

Neill Nutter

As the car pulled into the circular drive under a portico sheltering a massive wooden door, a handsome, slender woman of 50 plus years opened the door and spoke to the driver.

"I've been expecting you. Please explain what you want of me," she said.

It was obvious that they knew each other well.

He spoke quietly, but with a voice that resonated with authority, "I have a newborn child I want you to raise. He was abandoned earlier today in an alley."

"You want me to do what?" the women responded incredulously.

He replied, "I said, I have a baby that I want you to raise for me. I am not asking you to do this. I am telling you to do this. You owe me you know; you are in my debt. His name is to be 'Devadas.' Here are the adoption papers you must sign and the instructions for raising the child. He is to have your surname."

The woman's shoulders slumped, and her appearance changed for an instant from that of a wealthy, self-focused recluse to one of a servant required to do an onerous task.

For that brief moment Lady Ellen Smyth reviewed her life. She lived alone with only her servants. She had been born in a Liverpool ghetto, the product of a dysfunctional home. Her mother was an indifferent trollop and her father a ne'er do-well. Her relationship with that 'one' who brought the child began when she was a teen-ager. In her restless and unhappy youth, she had been drawn into the occult. Her involvement had grown to the point where, in desperation, she promised to do anything if she could be somebody and have wealth.

And it happened.

Edgar found her, or perhaps Ellen found him, when she was working in a pub. Edgar had gone abroad to personally attend to business. Alone and seeking company, he had gone somewhere he knew there would be people. His was the case of a lonely person meeting one whose entire life was focused on escaping her dead-end station in life, a 'bar girl' with little or no hope.

Ellen had no idea about the Edgar Smyth she had met across his several drinks. However, she knew instinctively that he was the solution to her 'Faustian' pledge. She didn't pry into his background or question his motives. He obviously had money, and that thought gave her the hope of freedom. Edgar was her winning ticket to the 'Irish Sweepstakes.' After an acquaintance of twenty-four hours and a half-dozen or so drinks, they were married.

Edgar Smyth had been very successful in the shipping business and had shrewdly invested a large portion of its earnings into petroleum exploration in the Middle East, the proliferation of casinos in Mediterranean resort areas, and the provision of arms and armament to would-be despots in the Middle East, Western Asia, and Africa. To say that he had amassed a great fortune would be an understatement. His wealth was never measured, for much came from quasi-legal pursuits that would never be recognized by 'Standard and Poor's.'

Now she controlled his nearly unlimited resources. She loved managing Edgar's money. His money was what she lived for. It gave her pleasure; it gave her a sense of freedom she had never known.

"Poor Edgar! So successful at attaining wealth, but unable to halt the spread of the cancer that took him in the prime of life." That thought made her smile inwardly, for he was gone, and it was all hers.

The visitor's irritation with her reverie was silent yet roused her back to the moment.

"How can this be?" She frowned deeply. "I have no interest or experience whatever with children. I don't like them, they don't like me, and I have Edgar's estate to manage."

Lady Ellen Smyth wanted little to do with people and had few friends. Social functions were held to a minimum and were attended only to impress. She made it a point to treat her help well, but it was because of self-interest, for a constantly changing staff would demand attention, and distract her from the financial management of her money, her interest and preoccupation.

He replied, "You have much wealth and many servants; you are intelligent and resourceful. You will find a way."

After a deep sigh of resignation and through clenched teeth, she responded, "Yes! I have help to feed, bathe and care for this waif, but I do not understand why I have been given this responsibility. I have the estate to manage."

He said nothing, but the expression in his eyes said the matter was settled. The woman feebly continued resisting as she signed the forms and accepted the instructions. "What will I tell my servants and my acquaintances?"

"What you tell anybody is your business. I have things to do. The baby is in a cardboard box in the trunk of the car. Call your servants, and get him out of there. He is a mess and hungry. If you let him die, I will make sure you have to explain to the authorities, and they will ask many questions. Now, hurry up. I have work to do." At that he got back in the car and released the trunk latch. The woman felt trapped, as indeed she was, and rued the day she had been so foolish.

She took a moment more to gather herself before squaring her shoulders and angrily going back into the house to call for help. By the time the butler and one of the maids appeared, the man had already started the car in his irritation.

The butler, following her instructions, lifted the trunk lid and took out the box. He set the box on the ground and closed the trunk. As the lid slammed shut, the car pulled away. And, as it did, the driver called out the window, "Remember your instructions. They are to be followed exactly – starting now." With that the car swiftly drove out the long drive and through the gate.

The woman and the two servants heard a weak cry from within the box and opened it, only to step back in horror at what greeted their eyes.

The maid was the first to react. "Oh my! This child needs attention and needs it now." And, with that, she tenderly lifted the messy, dirty, naked baby, held it to her bosom, and rushed into the building to her own quarters, leaving Lady Smyth – as she preferred to be called – and the butler.

"Hodge, take care of that box and mess, and I want no evidence of any of this left behind."

The maid, Hannah Desmaris, was 28 years old and the oldest of seven children. Plain, short, and plump, her appearance belied the force of her character, for she was a 'take charge' young woman, and the experience she had with six younger siblings gave her the wisdom and understanding of what needed to be done.

Once she was in her quarters, Hannah quickly filled the washbowl in her bathroom with lukewarm water. Then, while carefully holding the tiny baby, began to wash the dried blood and dirt off the child. The feel of water roused the child enough to cause him to again begin whimpering.

It had been some time since the baby had been found, and she had no idea how much earlier it had been abandoned. He was obviously very weak from hunger and exposure, so Hannah worked quickly, drying him with a soft towel and wrapping him with another. What could she feed him until proper baby formula could be obtained? Then she thought, "There is some sweetened condensed milk in the pantry. Perhaps a small amount would be all right, considering the circumstances." So, carrying the child, she quickly went to the kitchen.

"Eliza, I need help. Do we have any condensed milk?"

The cook turned toward her and exclaimed, "What in heaven's name are you holding?" and quickly moved closer. "Why, it's a baby!"

As the cook lifted the edge of the towel, one brief glimpse of the newborn's wan face set her into action. She rushed to the pantry, saw the cans of condensed milk, grabbed one and quickly opened it, put the milk in a cup, and warmed it in the microwave. Then she took a clean rag, twisted it into a nipple-sized twist, dipped it in the milk, and put it up to the baby's mouth. The baby needed no lessons on how to feed. It sucked hungrily on the improvised nipple and quickly consumed an ounce or two of the milk.

"That child is definitely a survivor," commented the maid. "The way he took to that milk was remarkable."

"I don't think we should give him any more," declared Eliza, "I'm afraid it will make him sick. We must send someone to get proper food for this child."

The maid nodded her head in assent and said, "Let me hold him. You go find Hodge or someone who is free and instruct him on what the child needs. You have raised your family and know what he requires."

The cook handed the infant to Hannah and, without a word, went to the kitchen telephone and dialed the butler's extension. It rang several times before he irritably answered, "Hodge."

The cook explained what she wanted and waited patiently while the butler calmed down and wrote the list of food, clothing, diapers, and other necessary items on his notepad.

"I don't understand at all what is going on around here," he remarked crossly.

"Well! That makes two of us. When Hannah hurried in to the kitchen with the baby all bundled up, she said that someone brought the baby to the house in a fancy car – someone the lady of the house obviously knew but didn't like."

The butler replied, "You should have seen what that child was in – an old, dirty cardboard box." He shuddered. "And he lay in a puddle of afterbirth. It was a nasty mess. The afterbirth went down the garbage disposal, and the box went in the incinerator. Where did the child come from anyway? Hmff! I'm on my way. I'll have Simms take me in the Buick."

As he hung up the phone, the cook heard him comment, "What is this world coming to?"

The servants were given total responsibility for the baby. Lady Smyth told them that his name was 'Devadas' and brushed all their questions aside. "You just keep your mouths shut. What people don't know won't hurt them. Furthermore," she said, "We have to keep this whole situation away from any authorities or any other busybodies."

Actually, the help knew nearly as much about the baby as Lady Smyth did, and they would receive the additional instructions soon enough. She did tell them that she was adopting the baby, and that he was to grow up on the estate as a favor to the man who brought him, in payment for a debt, but never explained further. That connection was a private matter, a matter she now regretted.

Fortunately for the child, the servants were a good lot. They accepted the additional responsibility somewhat grudgingly in the beginning, but the baby slowly and surely captured their heart, and they doted on him.

Only Lady Smyth remained aloof and indifferent. Taking on the responsibility of the child was only an obligation for an old agreement. She didn't have to be emotionally involved.

Chapter 2

LOVE TAKES ROOT

For the first four years the staff – the maids, the cook, the butler, gardener, and chauffer – cared for Devadas. Under their care and attention, he flourished and had the run of the entire estate. They would often shorten his name to 'Devad' and, occasionally, even to 'Dev.' Love and companionship were given him in abundance, and Devadas flourished. His desire to help in whatever was being done resulted in his being constantly underfoot which was accepted with gracious humor. Only his stepmother, Ellen Smyth, remained aloof and indifferent.

Devadas proved to be an unusually bright, gentle, sensitive little boy who blossomed with any and all attention. He loved the staff and was constantly at their heels asking all kinds of questions, questions about everything. His questions ranged from "Where do people come from?" to asking Simms, the chauffer, "Why is your hair red?" He wanted to know the names of everything: bugs, flowers, even the melodies that Fred Riley the gardener whistled, and he would try to whistle the way Fred did but with little success. The results were a warm, misty rush of air which frustrated him greatly.

The boy loved to draw and, when given a sheet of paper and a pencil, drew images of nearly every object at The Planes. From time to time one of the staff would help him by sharpening a pencil, or drawing his attention to something of especial interest. He seemed taken by natural things. He loved to draw leaves, flowers, trees, and people, his drawings revealing detail that most of the staff had never noticed. Color also fascinated him, and he would study a subject such as flowers – glads, dahlias, cosmos, and even the odd dandelion that had escaped Fred's crew – not missing a detail. It was a happy day when Hannah gave him his first set of colored pencils. He disliked felt-tip pens or crayons because they wouldn't show the detail he desired. And, if he could draw while listening to music, he would be content for hours.

Music was another of his passions. Whenever Devad would accompany Simms on an errand, he wanted to have music playing. While listening, he would sit quietly, silently humming, obviously lost in what he was hearing. Simms, who liked the company of the lad, was quick to oblige his request, for when the music was playing, Simms didn't have to answer the interminable questions that were the alternative.

Music was an important part of The Planes, and impromptu recitals were often held in the music room, as Ellen Smyth would at times have visitors that were musical. Mary Tompkins, her personal maid, was an accomplished pianist, having a degree in piano from the university.

Mary attended Ellen Smyth's every whim. She had grown up in a privileged home and was very knowledgeable about style and appearance. She was a tall, slender, erect woman, whom Lady Smyth had chosen because of her proper, quiet artistic temperament. She had excellent taste in clothes, the arts and propriety. She had married while at the university, but the marriage had been doomed to failure from the beginning. Unknown to her, her new husband had other interests and had married Mary for wealth and position. When she discovered his waywardness, she divorced him. In her despondency and frustration, she accepted the position of personal maid to Ellen Smyth.

Lady Smyth loved music and loved to have Mary play for her sometimes in the evening – especially after a difficult day – for while she seemed in good health, she suffered times of desolation, depression, and anxiety. Negative market changes would often affect her, but she also suffered from insomnia. When she was able to sleep, she had frequent and often violent nightmares.

When Mary would sit at the concert grand in the music room in the evening and play for Lady Smyth, Devadas, upon hearing the sounds of the great masters, would quietly slip into the great room and listen, his eyes glistening with delight as his mind processed the strains, rhythms and dynamics of the music.

Going for walks with Hannah was another activity that Devad loved, for she would tell him stories about herself when she was a little girl, and how she helped her parents with her brothers and sisters. This fascinated him, for having siblings or companions of similar age was a concept almost beyond his imagination. She would tell him about how she came to live and work at The Planes; and he especially liked the story about how he came to be one of theirs and how, when he was a tiny baby delivered to The Planes, Hannah had taken him in her arms and loved him.

It was also Hannah who would tuck him in at night, usually reading him a story which made bedtime special. Devadas loved Hannah, and there was a special bond between them, perhaps because she was the first one to have held him and shown him love.

Fortunately for all concerned, Devadas had good health and bypassed a lot of the childhood illnesses – probably in part because of his isolation – for Devadas had no contact with others his age except in his imagination. His was an adult world. His playmates were the staff – not because they entered into his world, for they had their responsibilities – but because they accepted him into their world. They were not put off by the bright, quick, oft-times precocious child, but would include him in their activities whenever possible.

The week before his fourth birthday, the one who had delivered Devadas was again a visitor at The Planes, and was seen in the library having a very serious discussion with 'The Lady Smyth.' The topic was the boy's education. The visitor was explaining that it was time for the boy's training to begin, for he had planned the boy's future in detail. He did not confide in Ellen Smyth about what he expected the boy to accomplish but said only that all their futures depended upon him.

"I have selected teachers and tutors to educate Devadas. All are indebted to me and will perform their duties flawlessly. We will begin the instruction on Monday of next week. You will pay for their services." Ellen Smyth began to object but quickly resumed her submissive role. The visitor noted her slight, but he said nothing. Only his eyes revealed the reprimand of her infraction. "The daily schedule will be as follows. The boy will arise at 7 am and have breakfast at 7:30 am. He will begin his lessons at 8:30 am and continue until noon. After lunch he is to have a rest period until 2:30 pm. At that time lessons will resume until 5 pm. After dinner he will be free, unless further study is required or special activities are planned by the teacher or tutor. At 9 pm he will get ready for bed. Bedtime is to be 9:30 pm. As the child becomes older, the educational expectations will be commensurate to his maturity and development."

"Weekends are to be devoted to cultural and educational activities such as visits to museums, theaters, art galleries etc. Religious expression is encouraged but is to be limited to groups tolerant of viewpoints that differ from their own. Narrowness and exclusivity will not be acceptable, for such ideas are counter-productive to what we have planned for the future."

"The child will have lessons for ten weeks, to be followed by an extended three week learning travel experience to areas of the world that will complement his education. It may be necessary for him at times to study abroad. Fluency in languages apart from English is essential, for I want this boy to be conversant in all the major world language groups, as well as to read Greek and Latin."

The plans presented seemed completely impossible to Lady Smyth, for she had little formal education and received most of what she knew in the "college of cruel experience," but her visitor was very shrewd and knew exactly what he was doing. From her past experience he was accustomed to getting his way. She was sure that his ambition and expectations for the boy would be carried out exactly as presented.

But what could he mean by the comment that "all their futures" depended upon the outcome? And weren't these plans too demanding? The whole idea seemed an impossible burden for the child and perhaps even for her and her staff.

The direction of her thinking had a curious effect on Lady Smyth. For the first time since the child had arrived four years earlier, she began to have a heightened concern for the youngster. The demands that were being placed on the boy awakened a spark of rebellion within her, and she was surprisingly irritated that a child so young should be placed in such a severe and even oppressive situation. She determined that her concern not show, for the one facing her was expert at reading body language and expression. Her care to cover her change in heart – be it ever so small – was successful, for her visitor looked down at his watch as if remembering another appointment and rose to leave.

"I will bring Devadas' first tutor a week from Monday, promptly at 8 am. You will have the classroom space prepared at that time. It must be world class. Spare no expense. I have been very generous with you. The facilities must be commensurate with the significance of the mission."

Lady Smyth was stunned. "A classroom area? A school, here in The Planes? I had no idea of the enormity of this – this project. However will I do this?"

Her guest narrowed his eyes with disdain. "You have money because I have given it to you. Now do as I say. I don't care how it's done, just do it."

As Lady Smyth showed her visitor to the door, she asked herself, "What am I doing? What is 'the mission' and how does our future depend upon it? Whatever does he mean? Why should he use the possessive pronoun "our"? And he wants an equipped school – here, at The Planes – done by a week from Monday? There isn't enough time. How can I do this? I have absolutely no experience either with children or their education. Whom will I get to help me do this?" and her mind filled with uncertainty as she closed the door behind her visitor. Her involvement with Devadas had just begun.

Little did she know how involved it would become.

∽

As Lady Smyth went to her quarters to freshen up before dinner, she had an inspiration. She would have Devadas eat dinner with her. "Mary!" she called her maid, "I would like Devadas to begin sharing his evening meal with me in the dining room. Tell Hannah to have him properly attired and instructed."

"Yes, Madam," replied Mary, surprised by this turn of events. Ellen Smyth, above all else, valued her privacy and, other than the soft strains of the great composers filling the room, wanted no noise or talking. Dining at the The Planes was a formal and solemn affair.

The dining room was large, nearly fifty feet long and about thirty feet wide. The ceiling was nearly twenty feet high and decorated with three complementing frescos and chandeliers. The floor was dominated by a great Oriental rug which was all but obscured by a massive long table flanked on both sides by a dozen chairs and, at each end, by a single, ornate chair. Sideboards lined the perimeter of the room. On one end of the room, in a prominent position, hung a portrait of Edgar, painted when he was about forty years old and shortly before he died. The walls were burgundy velvet with a gold design, accented by many paintings – landscapes and portraits.

When Lady Smyth dined, she sat alone at one end of the long table – the end on which hung Edgar's portrait. Hodge usually served her although, on occasion, Hannah or even Mary might have the honor. The rule was for nothing to be spoken. A nod of the head would suffice for most communication or sometimes a hand motion. The cook, Eliza, knew exactly what Madam liked and would vary the menu in small ways, as necessary, to prevent boredom. If Lady Smyth wished a change, she would inform either her secretary, Elizabeth Wood, or Mary, who would relay the request to the kitchen where Eliza, a master of the culinary arts, would adjust the menu accordingly. Eliza had been with the Smyths nearly as long as The Planes had been in the family.

Hannah had Devadas prepared for dining with Lady Smyth. To this date few words had passed between Lady Smyth and Devadas, for all the staff made an effort to distract Devadas whenever bent on any communication with the Lady. They knew that she did not wish to be bothered by the child who, up to now, had been at best an inconvenience. Devadas had eaten with the staff, and they had their own dining area where sometimes the conversations became pretty lively. Devad looked forward to meal times and the lighthearted banter that dominated most meals. That Devadas was a chatterbox was an understatement. Not only did he have all manner of questions, but he would also carry on a conversation with anyone who would humor him.

There were definitely big changes occurring at The Planes, and, this day, all the staff talked quietly about what was happening and why.

The dining room had always been off limits. As Hannah took Devad into the dining room, his eyes grew large as he looked around the enormous room and the food displayed very properly on the nearest sideboard. Hannah seated him to Lady Smyth's left, so he would not be distracted by looking out the great windows at the gardens and grounds outside. The crystal and china seemed so delicate that Devadas was frightened, lest he break something.

When Lady Smyth entered the dining room, Devadas was instructed to stand until she was seated at her regular place. As she sat down, she looked curiously at Devadas, almost as if seeing him for the first time.

Devad had been well prepared for eating with the Lady. He had been dressed in his best clothes and instructed how to use his napkin and silver. Consequently, he was unusually quiet and reserved and picked at the food that was placed before him. He missed being able to speak and the myriad discussions of the staff. He missed the freedom of eating with abandon – at least, with some abandon. After all, he was only four years old and trying to appear grown-up and proper was a lot to expect for a little boy.

Ellen Smyth broke her cardinal rule. She spoke to the boy. "I understand that my staff calls you Devad." The dam broke, and all Devadas' inhibitions disappeared. With a big smile he enthusiastically said, "James and Fred call me Dev, and you can too, if you like."

This outburst of warmth melted Lady Smyth's heart, and she said with a quiet smile, "Thank you! But I prefer to call you Devadas or Devad, and you are to call me Ellen." At that the soft music was lost in the eagerness of a small boy whose world was suddenly burst wide open. Hodge, who had been standing nearby waiting to attend to Lady Smyth's requests, allowed a slight smile, slipped quietly into the hall, and hurried to the kitchen.

The staff eating in the kitchen had heard the voices coming from the dining room and looked quizzically at Hodge as he came in. "You'll never believe what has happened. Come with me." And with that they followed him to the hall just outside the dining room, completely astonished at what they were hearing. As one, they shook their heads and quietly went back to their meal, smiling inside and out.

A bridge had been crossed, and there was no turning back. Ellen Smyth's denial of Devadas' existence in her home and in her life was over. They had instantly become friends. No! – more than that – they had become partners. Ellen Smyth's new role was to protect Devadas from whatever it was that their mutual antagonist was trying to accomplish. She had no idea what his ultimate goal might be, but she was now sure that his educational plan and goals were way too much for a small boy. For Devad's part, whether he knew it or not, his role was to slowly but surely break down the walls that Ellen had erected in her 55 years.

The evening's dinner with Devadas and the tangible but totally irrational sense of connecting caused Ellen Smyth to realize that she would no longer be a 'puppet' in the plans to create in the lad a role that she inherently knew would not benefit him, but only the one who brought him to The Planes. From now on, she would be proactive on Devadas' behalf, and the first matter of concern was the setting for his future education. Her desire was that it would be a warm, child-friendly atmosphere in which her charge would be content and happy.

Chapter 3
PREPARING FOR EDUCATION

It was evening, and Ellen Smyth had retired to her suite and sat exhausted in her favorite chair. As she relaxed, she reviewed the events of the day. The dinner with Devadas had been wonderful. Why had she been so distant toward the boy?

And there was her visit with the one who had brought Devadas to The Planes. What was he planning? And why did he say their futures depended upon the outcome? Then, her thoughts led to his demand that she provide an educational space, and by a week from next Monday, and world class? What was that about?

Providing such an environment for Devad was a task that Lady Smyth knew she could not do without help. That she had such a short amount of time was much more than an inconvenience, it was unreasonable and perhaps even impossible. Something had to be done right away. She needed a miracle. "But, miracles don't happen," she thought, "they have to be made."

How would she, or how should she proceed? Space would not be a concern, for there were many rooms in the manor that were not used, to minimize the necessity of their care and cleaning. Indeed, there was one suite of rooms – basically an apartment – on the third floor that might do very well. The rooms had excellent natural light and were quite spacious. In addition it had not one, but two toilets, so whether the tutor was a man or woman, there would be no conflict of bathroom facilities.

And money was not the issue. She knew that one can buy nearly anything, but this was not a case of 'stocks and bonds,' or 'food and clothing.' This was something that was completely alien to her experience.

After some thought she concluded that she should ask Mary for advice. Her personal secretary, Elizabeth, would not be available until the morning. Besides, she knew that Mary Tompkins was well educated, though she had paid little attention to what she had studied. She believed it had been music but was not sure.

Mary's social graces and understanding of the finer things of life, as well as her musical skills, would suggest that she might have insights into what Devad should have – at least what was needed to begin his education. Thus, she called Mary and asked if she would come to her drawing room.

When Mary knocked lightly on the door to her suite, Lady Smyth answered quietly from within. Mary entered to find the Lady, dressed in her robe and slippers, bent over her computer and muttering about the idiosyncrasies of the electronic age. As Mary stepped into the light, Lady Smyth sat back, looked up, and thanked her for coming at a time that was usually Mary's break from regular duties.

"I so appreciate your coming in, Mary. I am quite stymied by the request given me that I provide an adequate educational environment for Devadas and have it ready by a week from Monday. I really don't know about such things and thought you might be some assistance."

Mary Tompkins simply stared at her mistress for a moment with an expression that seemed to say, "Whatever are you talking about?" Instead she said, "I haven't thought about anything educational since my graduation from the university, and certainly not since my divorce. It was at that time that I came to work for Master Edgar. That was nearly 15 years ago. How can I help?"

At that comment, Ellen Smyth replied, "Well, it is certain that you have far more education than I, for I have none but 'infant school.' My mother wanted nothing to do with me other than to bring her a few shillings I might obtain by begging on the street – which I did, for it was better than sitting with those cruel and bad-tempered children in a classroom."

These words astonished Mary, for she had always assumed that Lady Smyth had come from a privileged background. Other than her preoccupation with stocks, bonds, and money in general, she always spoke in a refined manner and dressed and presented herself well.

Mary spoke slowly, but deliberately, "I do remember a little of my college years, but things have changed a great deal since I received my degree. Today's students use computers for nearly everything – for taking notes, tests, and giving presentations. I'm afraid that I am not at all familiar with what is happening in the field of education, and music is so different. We had hours of practice, but things academic were limited. Still, I do have a suggestion. You should talk to Fred Riley. Fred received his M.S. degree in horticulture just before coming here to manage the gardens. My B.A. was in music, but Fred's degrees are both in scientific fields which would be much more applicable to what Devad will probably study."

"I will! That is an excellent suggestion. I'll call him right now," said Lady Smyth as she picked up the phone and dialed the number of the cottage where Fred lived with his buff colored Cocker Spaniel 'Taffy.'

It was after 9 pm when Fred received the call. "Riley, here!"

She could hear faint strains of music in the background. It sounded like jazz. "Fred, this is Ellen Smyth. I need some help."

That Lady Smyth should call him at all, using her first name and at this hour, was unheard of. "O.K.," he responded in a drawn-out quizzical voice, "What can I help you with?"

"It's about Devad."

"Is the kid all right?" Fred spoke with a note of anxiety.

"Oh, Devad's fine. You, perhaps, have heard that he is going to begin his schooling soon."

Fred said, "No, I haven't heard anything about that. He always has his endless questions, but he's never said anything about going to school. He was just helping me plant some of the annuals, but he didn't say anything to me about it. I see him quite often because he likes to play with Taffy. It's quite the love affair."

Lady Smyth laughed, and continued, "Well, I must have school rooms ready a week from Monday when Devad's first tutor will arrive." She didn't provide any explanation as to why this was necessary, but only addressed the urgency.

Although Fred Riley kept to himself, his gardens and his dog, he was a keen observer of human nature. And he had noticed with considerable interest, that Lady Smyth had changed after Devadas had come to The Planes. Before, she had been very direct and almost arrogant. But, since the boy had been here, she was more cautious, less sure of herself, maybe more thoughtful, and certainly preoccupied. It was if someone, or something else, was directing her activities.

Besides, where had the child come from? Why did his arrival so upset the status quo of the estate? It wasn't a bad thing. Actually, Dev brought a life to The Planes that had never existed before he came. These thoughts rushed through his mind, paralleling the statement – or was it a question – about the need to have an educational space in the 'castle,' his name for the manor.

"I don't understand what this has to do with me," Fred finally answered.

Lady Smyth sighed, and said, "I don't know where to begin, and Mary suggested that you might have some ideas."

"Please explain. Maybe then I'll understand better what you want," said Fred.

Lady Smyth sighed again and said, "I have been directed by the one who first brought Devadas to The Planes, and to whom," (and she paused before continuing), "I am deeply indebted, to provide for Devad's education. The teachers will be assigned, but I have to establish the 'physical plant,' as it were, where the teaching will take place. I don't know how to proceed, and Mary suggested that you might have at least an idea how to begin."

"Oh! Now I understand. You want some suggestions on how to get started. Well, I have a couple of ideas - off the top of my head. When I was an undergraduate, I considered going into teaching, so took some education classes. My favorite prof was a super fellow who even made Philosophy of Education interesting to me, for at that time if it wasn't science, I could have cared less. I think he is still at the University. I'm sure he would have some ideas on how to proceed."

"No, no, no! That will never do. Someone like that will have too many questions, and I can't have anybody prying into why we have the child, where he came from, and why we, rather, I am raising him. I simply can't go that direction."

"Well, the only other thing I can suggest is a school or educational supply store that may have consultants or know of somebody that might help you develop and equip such a facility. But Monday next week? That isn't much time. Tomorrow is Friday. I don't know how you can possibly do what you want to do in the time that you have. It will take a miracle."

"Do you know of such a place? Of course I can have Elizabeth look tomorrow in the Yellow Pages."

"Well, there is an educational supply store in the mall near the expressway. I go to the mall to see a movie from time to time. I seem to remember that it is quite close to the theater. Let me find it in the telephone book, and call you back with the number and the location."

"Thank you,' Lady Smyth replied, "If this doesn't work, I don't know what I will do."

In a few minutes, Fred Riley called back with the number and location. "The store is called 'Creative Learning,' and the ad in the Yellow Pages says they open at 10 am." Fred quickly added, "I hope they can help."

It was the next morning and a Friday. Elizabeth Wood, Ellen Smyth's secretary, was in the office working at her desk when Lady Smyth came in. She explained to Elizabeth, who had been with the Smyths for nearly 25 years, what she wanted to do and asked that Elizabeth call the school supply store precisely at 10 am. "It is called 'Creative Learning.' Here is the phone number and location. When you get them, I would like to talk to the manager."

When the phone was answered, Elizabeth asked, "May I speak to the manager?"

"Speaking," he replied.

"Just a moment," she said, and Lady Smyth picked up her phone.

"My name is Ellen Smyth, and I have a rather odd and unusual, yet urgent request. I wish to establish something . . . . . , something . . . . . .," (she had difficulty explaining what it was she wanted without giving too much information) "where young children can be taught in an environment conducive to learning."

"You mean something like a learning center?" the manager suggested.

"Yes, that's it, a learning center."

"How many children would this be for?" asked the manager.

"Oh, the number isn't important, but it would be small. It is the quality and diversity of materials that are important to me."

The manager of Creative Learning paused. "I recently heard of a school here in the city that closed at the end of the past school year. It was patterned somewhat after a Montessori school, but with more of an emphasis on directed academics, especially the classics. The founders of the school overextended themselves, and their debt load became so high they couldn't make the payments. Are you interested in a building as well?"

"No, I just need the equipment and materials."

"Well, this might work, for my understanding is that the building they used was rented. Just a minute, I wrote down the number of whom to call; it is here somewhere."

Ellen Smyth's eyes glistened. "This is too good to be true," she thought.

After a few brief seconds, the manager's voice said, "Yes! Here it is," and gave Lady Smyth the phone number.

She thanked him and, immediately after hanging up, personally dialed the number he had given her.

"Genesis Mortgage," a female voice answered, "May I help you?"

"Yes, please. I am inquiring about a school that had to close because of bankruptcy. It is my understanding that all the equipment and materials might be available?"

"Just a minute please, Mr. Gleason handles those matters. He is in this morning. I will connect you to his extension."

"Gleason here. May I help you?"

"Yes, please! My name is Ellen Smyth," and she repeated the question she had just asked the receptionist.

"Yes, I seem to remember that school foreclosure. It was called 'Awakening Minds School for the Gifted,' or something like that. I have that file on my computer. Let me bring it up. Ah yes, here it is. I was right, and I had the right name. The information I have says that the school was only in operation for two seasons. Pity that, but the organizers way overextended, and we had to take possession of all their assets. It is right here in the city. We have advertised all over the country but so far no one has expressed any interest in buying the property as a unit. Some have expressed interest in this or that, but we want to try to sell everything as a package."

Lady Ellen Smyth was elated, for this seemed the answer to their needs, and she quickly struck a deal with Genesis Mortgage company that was especially generous, certainly not Lady Smyth's usual manner, with the contingency that possession of the equipment and materials could be accomplished early next week, and no questions asked.

Mr. Gleason had been taken aback by the suddenness of the sale, but because a liability for the company had suddenly become a sizable benefit, he moved quickly to their mutual benefit.

Lady Smyth instructed Elizabeth to proceed with the purchase and to make arrangements to pick up and transport all to the estate.

As Ellen Smyth sat back in her desk chair, she reflected on the events of yesterday and today. Since that individual to whom she was personally indebted had first brought the baby, her life was becoming increasingly complicated, and she somewhat resented not being in control. She had begun a relationship with a four-year old boy that on the one hand brought meaning to her life, but on the other hand posed challenges she could never have imagined. The Devadas affair was bigger than she was; it was becoming obvious that she and the staff would all have to work together. They had already included Devad in their hearts, so they had a vested interest in the boy's future.

Lady Smyth made a decision. "Elizabeth, I think we should have a meeting with all the staff this afternoon and the earlier the better. What do you think of all of us meeting in the library at 2 pm?"

Twice Chosen

"That is very short notice," Elizabeth retorted. "Some may have previous commitments."

"Well! We shall get by with those who are able to attend," and she left the room to go upstairs to the apartment area she was considering for the 'school.' She would have to be quick because lunch was served precisely at 12:30 pm.

All the staff was gathered in the library before Lady Smyth arrived – surprisingly. The Bedells, Eliza the cook and her husband Jeb the maintenance chief, were sitting at the large table, discussing why they were having a meeting and with such short notice. Jeb, still wearing his baseball cap with big black letters spelling "**CAT**" was openly fussing about having to come in when he had so much to do. He was loud and a bit uncouth, always seen in jeans held up by suspenders and that ubiquitous yellow hat. Today, he had at least a day's growth on his face which didn't add much to his appearance. Putting that aside, Jeb was an excellent craftsman – not easy to work for, for nothing but perfection was acceptable – and a curious enigma, considering his appearance and manner. He had a crew of a half dozen or so who together maintained the physical plant of The Planes in fine order.

Hannah – young, short and plump, with twinkling eyes – was standing, looking out the window, watching some squirrels chasing each other across the lawn. Mary, quietly humming a strain from Gershwin's 'Porgy and Bess,' was fussing over a bouquet that was on a sideboard.

Fred Riley and James Simms were chatting together and perusing the shelf with current issues of magazines. James was thumbing through an issue of "Classic and Sports Car Magazine' – a monthly British publication. James owned an immaculate, green 1948 MG-TC – his pride and joy – and was keenly interested in such things. Fred had found a copy of 'Southern Living.' Their interests held part of their attention but left room for discussing the intent of the meeting. Fred was telling James of his call from Lady Smyth the night before and expressing his opinion that the meeting had to have something to do with Dev.

John Hodge, the butler, was sitting by himself at the long table, wiping his glasses with his handkerchief and glad for the opportunity to sit down and rest. He had been cleaning the silver in the dining room that morning and was very content with a moment's peace.

Elizabeth Wood was also sitting at the large table, across from John, and making sure the digital recorder was working properly. She recorded all meetings to keep an accurate record of all business and related subjects. Elizabeth never left anything to chance and prided herself on her attention to detail.

As Lady Smyth entered the room, the discussions ceased; those standing sat down, and all faces turned expectantly toward her.

"As you probably have guessed, this meeting concerns Devadas. I asked one of the girls in the kitchen to keep an eye on him for us as we were meeting.

"I have been instructed by Devadas' 'benefactor' to begin his education and have an area where this will take place. He gave me no details about what we should have or where it is to be placed, only that it is to be of the highest quality and ready by a week from Monday – very short notice, since this is Friday."

"The timing has been remarkable, for just this morning I found out about a school for gifted children that became seriously arrears in its payments and had to be sold to pay its creditors. That this has happened is nearly a miracle; because I don't believe that miracles exist, I will simply call it 'good fortune.'"

"You all are already very fond of the lad, and I too, as of last evening, have been captured by his sweet innocent manner. Oh, I am not saying he doesn't get into mischief from time to time, for I have heard the stories told by Eliza – like the time he was caught climbing the shelves in the pantry to get to the cookies, or drawing on the mirror in Hannah's apartment with her lipstick, and there are many more – but, for some reason, recently I have been strangely drawn to him, and I can't explain it."

She paused a moment.

"Back to his education! From what I have had outlined for me, it seems far too rigorous and demanding for the boy. I'd like to intervene, but we. . . . ., I can't really control the process per se, but we can be aware of what is taking place and perhaps be there for him – at least emotionally, and to lessen the pressure – if possible. What I am saying is don't be hesitant to express your love to Devad. He is, after all, just four years old and never had his own parents to love and care for him, and we must step in and fill the void."

"I'm a novice at expressing love, but I'm sure I can learn – and, perhaps, you can help me in the meantime. Thank you for all that you have done to raise the boy and for all the contributions you have made, even with the demands I've placed upon you. I, myself, have been so indifferent, whereas you have been so active."

"Thank you so much!"

"The main reason I have brought you together is that through Fred's help, the equipment and materials were found that will enable us to convert an area of the manor into a real school. Perhaps you remember there is a suite of rooms on the third floor that have been closed since my husband passed away. I would like to use those rooms and adapt them for the 'learning center.' The space has 4,000 to 5,000 square feet, wonderful light and most adequate bathroom facilities."

"I would like to have James take Jeb, Fred and Mary to the building where all the furniture and other materials are stored, and for you to take inventory, photos, videos, measurements and anything else that is necessary and bring these details back so that we can decide how to best use the area selected. All will not fit in the space, for the school had about 12 students in each of four classrooms, and we have just Devad. Many items will have to be stored, sold, or disposed of in some other manner. Elizabeth has made arrangements for a moving company to move these things right after the weekend. Our time is short – only a week. I would like the area to be child-friendly – cozy, light, bright, and inviting but not cluttered. The furniture that is already in the rooms can be taken out and placed in our storage area. I would like all of you to help in this."

"Are there any questions?"

There were questions, and for some she had no answers, but all those present seemed enthusiastic about the project with the possible exception of Jeb, who had too many projects already. Most of what was being asked was in the planning and advising realm. There was plenty of other staff to do the hard grunt work. Thankfully, there were two service elevators for the building that would simplify the job of getting the furniture, equipment, and materials to the classroom area.

The classroom furniture, computers, whiteboards, books, educational toys, etc., were in excellent condition, considering two years' use. Awakening Minds School for the Gifted had been designed for a K-8 curriculum with four classrooms and a maximum of a twelve students in each. There was way more than The Planes could possible use, and what to do with the extras was a challenge. The materials included thousands of books and reference materials, many in multiples, and "this was" the negative side of buying an entire school. The positive side allowed them to select the best of everything, so what they had was essentially new with lots of backup as needed.

Everyone worked diligently to get the area ready for use – even to wiping and washing everything with disinfectant to guard against introducing any unnecessary illnesses.

When all the materials were sorted to a one-child size school, everything was easily fit into the selected space. Jeb had his crew improve the lighting and, with input from Hannah, Mary and Fred, paint the rooms in child-friendly colors, install window treatment and make sure the bathrooms were working properly. The carpeting was replaced. A lab bench with all the necessary hardware, including proper ventilation, was installed. To complete the job, two computer carrels with state-of-the-art computers and a sound and video projection system were installed.

The week passed too quickly, and extra hours were spent to make sure all was ready for the tutor and the beginning of Devadas' education.

༄

It was early Monday morning before sunrise when Ellen roused. She had been dreaming, not the nightmare variety, but the frustrating kind - something she repeatedly could not accomplish. When fully awake the uncomfortable feeling that something was wrong, very wrong gripped her heart though she did not know what it was.

Now she was fully awake and apprehensive about the arrival of the tutor for Devadas who would be brought by the one who brought Devadas four years before. Her dream must have had some connection to this, for it seemed an extension of the discomfort with which she had awakened.

As she lay in bed, her apprehension became a sense of foreboding – not just for now but for the future as well. Ellen Smyth had been a creature of self-encapsulation. She had been so self-oriented, she was a 'black hole' of self-absorption. All her life had been about money. Anything or anybody that grew close to her was in danger of being drawn in and annihilated by her preoccupation. She was almost an extension of that one to whom she was indebted, but now had begun to be aware of her self-centeredness. And it all began but a few days before when she had been joined by a small child at her dinner table.

It was as though she had been in a dark room, perhaps a cell, but since last evening in the dining room, something or someone had caused the wall around her to crack, and an intense beam of light had penetrated her space. She had never before experienced anything like this. But the light that entered her world showed it as distasteful and ugly. She didn't understand this at all, but that same bit of light also warmed something within her and gave her hope, something she had never before experienced or understood. She knew that in some way all this involved the boy.

But why was she so anxious? She hurriedly did her bath and dressed, but it was only now beginning to become light. What was she going to do until Mary brought breakfast to her room? It wouldn't be ready for another hour. Television brought scant relief. Early morning television programming was depressing. In her channel surfing, she quickly bypassed a TV evangelist saying something like, "Our hope is in Jesus. . . ." The name of Jesus had always been a curse to her ears, but the word "hope" resonated within her.

Twice Chosen

Ellen Smyth picked up a magazine, a current issue of 'Movers and Shakers,' but nothing there registered anything in her mind but indifference, and callousness. She then opened up her notebook computer and, using her ID and password, spent a moment studying her assets and scanning her investments and their growth, but this, too, seemed a waste. What was happening to her? It all centered on Devadas, a four-year old boy foisted on her four years ago. Ellen Smyth's world was being shaken and she was miserable with uncertainty.

No! She was not miserable. She had been given a responsibility, something that had meaning, something good, a mission. Her change of outlook embraced even her staff. She was seeing her world in a new light.

Lady Smyth drifted aimlessly from her private suite and then, in a more deliberate manner, walked down the hall to the stairway to the third floor. There she proceeded to the classroom area where Devadas would receive his education. As she entered, she turned on all the lights and warmed to the bright colors, the shelves lined with books, the computers, desks and tables, and the toys selected to increase a child's imagination and shape his future. There were pictures on the walls and maps and charts.

As she examined the area, she paused here and there touching the various objects, seeing all with eyes that had never beheld anything like this. She was beside herself with joy and disbelief. It was all dreamlike, and it was all for her Devadas.

What had she just thought? Her Devadas? She was mad; she had become completely crazy, irrational, and out of control. Her Devadas? She had better get that idea out of her head and fast.

Her benefactor. . . . . ., no, her antagonist, and the tutor would be here in less than two hours, and he would never tolerate such a perspective. People were objects to be manipulated and used. Such feelings as love and concern were for the weak.

But the sense of concern for Devadas, his education, and his future reasserted itself within her, and her frown changed to a smile as she considered the boy and her new role.

She went to the elevator to return to the second floor. She was quite sure that Mary had brought her breakfast by now and would probably be waiting, worried because of her absence.

And she was right.

Chapter 4

LEILY BORHAN

Ellen Smyth was in her office when Elizabeth got the call from the gate phone that they had arrived. She immediately went to the drawing room, knowing that Hodge would greet their guests and bring them there. She wanted to make an impression of dignity and grace for the tutor. First impressions were important, though she somehow knew that whomever her one-time benefactor brought to teach Devadas would have little regard for such things.

When Hodge brought in the two visitors, Lady Smyth was idly paging through a large coffee-table book with pictures of the Mediterranean area. She rose from where she had been sitting and went forward to greet them.

Ellen Smyth's eyes grew large as she approached to shake hands with the new tutor. The woman carried two large suitcases, if she was indeed a woman. She was large, although her figure was obscured by a dark colored jilaabah and a headscarf. The initial impression was that she was built like a football lineman. She had to be over six feet tall and, with the jilaabah, appeared built something like a tree. The way she carried her two suitcases suggested that she was all muscle. She wore no make-up, her face was puffy, her eyes appeared dark and deep-set, and she wore a perpetual scowl. Her age was indeterminable.

As they shook hands, her companion said, "This is Leily Borhan. Ms. Borhan is from the country of Iran. Her undergraduate education was completed in Iran. Since then, she received her M.S. in elementary education and Ph.D. in classical studies from Bridgeford University. She has minors in anthropology and simian behavior. She has over 20 years of teaching experience, so she is well prepared to teach the boy. She has presented numerous papers and published several books; the subject of her last book is 'Persian Early Education.' She will tolerate no misconduct or mischief."

Leily Borhan responded to the introduction with a nod and a slight bow. "Lady Smyth!"

Her voice, despite her appearance, was very young and feminine. She spoke very good English with only a hint of accent. Her visage and voice were incompatible. Strange! Something seemed amiss.

Her escort quickly went on, "Ms. Borhan will be living here at The Planes for the duration of her tenure. I have a contract that you will sign listing salary and housing arrangements, so that everything will be legal and done to my satisfaction."

"Now, I would like to take Ms. Borhan to the teaching area, so she can see where she will be teaching. You do have it ready, I presume."

"Oh yes, we have it ready, but I'm not sure that Ms. Borhan will be happy staying here." This statement translated that Ellen Smyth would not be happy with Ms. Borhan staying there.

"You have no say about that, for she will be staying here. Now, while I am here, take us to the education area and to where Ms. Borhan will be staying, preferably close to where she will be teaching."

Ellen Smyth was not happy having Ms. Borhan on the premises, but what could she say? She was again regretting her decision made so long ago. The arrangement with her supposed benefactor definitely had its downside.

They took an elevator to the third floor and walked the short distance to the classroom area. As Lady Smyth led them in, Ms. Borhan grunted a sound that expressed disbelief. "Where did you get those colors? And these carpets - this will never do. This is much too, a. . . a. . . 'frivolous.' This isn't a teaching space, this is a. . . a. . . party room. I am here to educate the young man, not to entertain him. A child would be much too distracted here. And those windows, do they open? I hope not! We must have covers over them. Trees and sunlight and. . . and. . .and. . . we can't have that."

Lady Smyth was nearly beside herself. She straightened to her full five feet six inches, threw her shoulders back and announced, "There is no way that we will make any changes to these educational facilities. My staff and I have gone to considerable expense and effort to obtain, equip, and decorate these premises, and I will not change a thing. Additional materials and equipment will be considered on an item-by-item basis, but no other changes will be allowed. Requests will be given to my secretary, Elizabeth Wood, who will study them and present them to me with her recommendation."

Ellen Smyth was shocked at what she had just said, so unlike her usual measured manner of speaking.

With a "Harrumph," Ms. Borhan declared, "I don't believe I wish to work here."

The patron said simply, "You will," and turned to Lady Smyth with a look that suggested that he would deal with her later.

"Well! Where is my room?" said Ms. Borhan, the tone of her voice demanding.

Lady Smyth said flatly, "I was not aware that staying here was part of the plan. We do have many rooms, so you probably can find one to your liking."

Ms. Borhan stated brusquely, "I would like to be in a room facing east or north, preferably east, toward Mecca. I do not like sunshine, or flowers, or trees, so I would prefer something with minimal view."

At this suggestion Lady Smyth smiled to herself and spoke optimistically, "There is such a room on the top floor used primarily for storage, but it has a bathroom and closet. Its only window is small and faces the north, not the east. All our rooms with an eastern exposure face the gardens. Directly below this room are the workshops and a parking area. You will not see gardens or sunlight from that window. It will be a bit noisier because of activity in the area below, but there are no rooms in The Planes that have much noise because of the thickness of the walls and the interior finishing."

Her inward smile quickly changed to a frown as she thought, "What kind of strange person is this woman? What is her agenda?" She would alert her staff to watch this new teacher closely, thinking, "We must protect Devadas."

Leily Borhan seemed pleased with the proposed room, its exposure, and privacy. The fact that it won her approval added to Lady Smyth's concern. After Ms. Borhan set her bags in the room, she said, "Now I want to meet the young man. First impressions are very important."

The three then returned to the classroom.

When they arrived, Mary and Elizabeth were already there with Devadas, who had been underfoot during the move and redecorating, but who had not seen the completed project. He was exploring every nook and cranny – opening this, touching that, sitting at the desks, looking out the windows, turning the lights on and off. The little boy was curious about everything.

The moment the three of them stepped in the classroom area, Devadas quickly moved as far away as possible. He likely would have escaped into the hall had the newcomers not been standing in the doorway. What caused his reaction wasn't clear, but it wasn't shyness, for Devadas was not shy. The look in his eyes was one of fear.

"Come here, Devad, and meet your new teacher," said Lady Smyth. Devadas ducked under a desk and wouldn't move. "Come here, Devadas. You must meet Ms. Borhan. She is going to teach you how to read and work with numbers."

Apparently Devadas was not impressed, for he made himself as small as he could, hoping the two newcomers would leave.

"Come out, Devadas. I won't hurt you. I want to be your friend; I want to help you learn to read books and use the computer. I want you to like me. In fact I want you to love me."

Her words curdled Ellen's heart. That voice. . . . .

At the continued encouragement of Ms. Borhan, Devadas peeked out from behind the desk, at which time Lady Smyth gently took him by the hand and alternately lifted and pulled the little boy from his retreat into the room to meet his teacher.

"Devadas, I want you to meet Ms. Borhan." Devad held out his hand to shake hers but, after touching her, quickly pulled back and became very reticent to do more. He muttered something, tried to pull away, but was unsuccessful, for Lady Smyth still firmly held his other hand.

The entire introduction was at best awkward and, curiously, no introduction was made to the companion of Ms. Borhan. Devad would have nothing to do with him and avoided even looking at him. It was as if he remembered him, and that memory brought a sense of great fear and loathing.

After the introduction, Ms. Borhan's escort made some comment about other appointments and left. There was no goodbye, no good luck, no well wishes of any kind, and all those present except for the new tutor, whose reaction they could not fathom, were very relieved when he left the room. Neither Mary nor Elizabeth offered to see him out. He simply left.

Ms. Borhan said, "I must go to my room for materials to use in working with Devadas. I will return in a few minutes. Then we can become acquainted and get started with his education." With that she left the room.

Devad said, "I don't like her." The others looked at one another with looks of total agreement.

"Mary, I would like you to stay here with Devadas and Ms. Borhan, at least for today. Watch for anything that would or could be used to send her out of here to wherever she came from." Mary nodded her head in agreement.

Lady Smyth, who still held Devad's left hand, reached out and took the other hand, and said, "Devad, I want you to do what Ms. Borhan says. You will be all right; we will be nearby," though in her heart she wasn't sure. "Do you understand me? Mary will be here with you today. This is a new beginning, and beginnings are always hard." And with that she impulsively kneeled down and kissed Devad on the forehead.

What had she done? She hadn't kissed anyone since Edgar had passed away, and those kisses had been usually cursory at best.

The imposing Ms. Borhan returned with a large, shiny black briefcase. She had removed her outer covering. Her clothes were more like that of a man, and not one bit feminine, though they were of obvious high quality. She wore dark brown slacks, a dark red blouse, and brown oxfords. Her hair was black and cut short. She appeared nearly as imposing in western dress as she did when first seen in the jilaabah and headscarf.

She opened her briefcase, removed a great many papers, and set the case by the desk. "Devadas, come sit on this chair beside me. I want us to become acquainted. I want to ask you some questions. We need to get to know each other."

She sat down.

"Devad, do you mind if I call you Devad?" He nodded yes - reticently.

Lady Smyth and Elizabeth rose to go, and Ms. Borhan, with a shake of her head acknowledged their leave. As they walked out the door, Lady Smyth turned her head and said, "Mary will stay with you today, so that Devadas will be more at ease." No objection was raised, so the two of them disappeared down the hall toward the elevator.

Ms. Borhan carefully laid out the papers on her desk and began asking Devadas questions. Mary noted almost immediately that Devadas was being given an IQ test of some kind. Devad quickly rose to the task and often added related details and ideas. Ms. Borhan listened intently to his answers without comment but made many notes, nodding her head from time to time as he spoke. The questions were very probing, and Devadas' answers were coherent, thoughtful and demonstrated great intellect.

By the time the session was over, it was time for lunch, and Devad quickly bounded from his chair, ran from the room, and headed for all his friends in the dining room. Mary lingered for a moment, looking quizzically at Leily Borhan who sensed her questioning gaze. "I think we have a prodigy on our hands," she said. "Incredible!"

In spite of the odd appearance and behavior of Leily Borhan, she was able to teach. And while Devadas didn't especially like his teacher, he tolerated her, for she was his vehicle on the road to knowledge. The same intensity with which he pursued everything was now focused on learning.

But Leily Borhan had her problems with Devadas. The first was that she could hardly keep up with his ability to absorb whatever it was she presented. The second was that at times he seemed lost in another world.

Many times when she was working through a lesson, she would notice his eyes drift into another dimension, and he would begin quietly humming some musical refrain or picturing a score of a melody played only in his mind.

And again, Devadas would sometimes be sketching in his notebook - something he had seen at the museum, on the grounds of the estate, or maybe on one of the trips he had taken with staff or Lady Smyth. At other times, he would be looking out a window and watching the clouds, the movement of trees, or the flight of birds. These were not times of daydreaming, drifting into the world of his imagination, but the analysis of what he saw; the beauty of movement, shape and color.

These breaks in the flow of learning frustrated Ms. Borhan's determination to hold his attention to the subject at hand, and often she could be heard grumbling about the windows, the play of sun and shadow across the gardens or lawn of The Planes, and the effect they seemed to have on Devadas.

In spite of her lament about Devadas' distractions, they did not slow his absorption of detail, and she could only wonder at the rate of his progress. The boy was gifted, and she was determined to move him as fast as she could.

Reading, grammar and basic math were disposed of in short order, and soon the boy was jointly working on learning Greek, Latin, Arabic, mathematics, geography and science. His ability to comprehend and process diverse and difficult material was remarkable.

Since Leily Borhan was Iranian, she was fluent in Farsi and Arabic as well as English, French and German. She counted many friends in the Middle Eastern world and was a devout Muslim. Hence, she was kindly disposed to the plight of the Palestinian people.

One of Leily Borhan's goals was to lead Devadas into Islam, that great faith that she clung to tenaciously. Devadas became her personal Jihad, and she lauded the culture and peoples of the Middle East.

Ms. Borhan especially liked the poetry of Mahmoud Darwish, and had Devadas, when quite young, memorize the poem, 'Identity Card," along with other selections.

Once she had him recite the poem for Ellen Smyth. This took place in the drawing room of The Planes. Devadas stood stock still and, looking straight ahead, spoke solemnly:

"Identity Card"

"Record!

I am an Arab

> And my identity card is number fifty thousand
> I have eight children
> And the ninth is coming after a summer
> Will you be angry?
> Record!
> I am an Arab
> I have a name without a title
> Patient in a country
> Where people are enraged . . ."

"All right, Devad, explain to Lady Smyth what thought that poem is expressing." And Devadas explained how the nation of Israel had begun, and how the indigenous people – the Palestinians – had lost their homeland.

"Would you now recite the poem in Arabic, please? I just love to hear the language, and Devadas pronounces the words so well."

Throughout the ensuing months, Leily Borhan had Devadas study Arabic— almost to the exclusion of anything else. He learned much Arabic poetry and memorized lengthy portions of the Koran.

Yasser Arafat was a hero of Leily Borhan, and Devadas was required to learn many quotes. One such quote was:

"Whoever stands by a just cause cannot possibly be called a terrorist."

These thinly veiled attempts to bring Devadas to a particular religious or political persuasion were not effective. He viewed the literature read, the languages learned, and the writings memorized as parts of the whole of his education. And he had the amazing capacity to analyze and synthesize information, fitting in what he was learning with what he had already learned, keeping it impersonal. Besides, social studies, economics and politics, while interesting, were only that— interesting - for he loved music and art. These were what captured and held his attention.

Mary Tompkins helped Devadas learn to play the piano. She taught him technique and provided him with music appropriate for his level. She had him sit with her at the piano, praising and correcting him as necessary, and often encouraged him to play along with her.

Listening to music with Mary helped sharpen his listening skills, and it helped him recognize the subtleties that composers weave into their music.

Whenever convenient, she would take him to the University to hear recitals, afterwards reviewing what they had heard and evaluating the performance's strengths and weaknesses.

Devadas found rhythms and harmonies multi-dimensional. His world was not flat. It was instead a three-dimensional tapestry of sounds, with their colors and nuances all dancing together but with disparate motions, yet alike – something like a brook weaving through a wood or meadow. He liked all music but not equally. He was especially fond of the freedoms found in Gustav Mahler, George Gershwin, Ottorino Respighi, Dave Brubeck and Thelonius Monk, but equally loved the structure of Bach and Mozart. His least favorite music was that which was loud and electronically amplified to jet engine intensity.

Devadas would play the piano when emotionally energized, relaxing, or when entertaining. He loved playing for an audience as much as the audience enjoyed listening to him, and his favorite audience was Ellen Smyth. Often after the dinnertime, Devadas and his adopted mother would go to the music room where she would sit quietly with her eyes aglow as he played for her. He was a born entertainer.

'The Planes' for all intents and purposes, was a veritable art museum of an unusually high quality. When Edgar traveled in Europe, Africa and Asia, he collected a considerable amount of painting, sculpture, tapestries, and other pieces that he liked. Devad would, when the opportunity arose, sit on a chair in front of a piece he admired and analyze what he liked and disliked about it. As his skills developed, he would try to emulate what he had seen with increasingly credible results.

He found the French impressionists pleasant, but especially liked the works of those who painted nature, such as Audubon, Basil Ede, Martin Koch, and Robert Bateman. Charlie Russell was one of his all time favorites, because his works contain so much movement and drama, with each painting telling a story.

Devadas began drawing as soon as he could hold a crayon or a pencil. By the time he was three, he could draw recognizable objects and, when he was about five, began to experiment with watercolors. Fred Riley had taken some art as an undergraduate and helped Devadas get started. Fred had quite a portfolio of watercolors he had done of flowers, and his efforts inspired Devad to emulate him.

Devadas was not one to splash on paint – at least without purpose. You might say that he was a literalist, for his interests were to accurately portray what he saw in form and in color. He would see every shade and nuance.

This attention to detail was an extension of his personality but, at the same time, he could by a stroke of the pencil or brush demonstrate to the viewer a sense of involvement in the art.

Ellen Smyth loved to accompany him to the library or perhaps the classroom area where she would admire and wonder at his drawings. His artwork had become quite accomplished, if that was the best description. It was beautiful. His drawing of trees and clouds gave the impression of movement, grace, line, and proportion.

Leily Borhan could not understand Devadas' preoccupation with the arts. She had a mission, and had come to The Planes with that purpose. To have that mission diluted by the likes of Beethoven, Debussy, Michelangelo, Monet, Renoir, and the like frustrated and displeased her. She did her best to distract this characteristic of his personality, believing that a person could be dissuaded, or at least discouraged, by rewarding sought after behaviors while penalizing the undesirable ones.

Her application of this 'Skinnerian' psychology didn't work. Actually, it may have had a negative effect on her desire to woo him to her 'World View.' Had she incorporated the arts, apart from the poetry and other rhetoric she imposed upon Devadas, she might at least have achieved a sympathetic acceptance of her perspective. Instead, Devadas politely tolerated her idiosyncrasies and vigorously pursued his love and fascination for all things that caused his heart to sing.

Chapter 5
WEEKENDS AND BREAKS

Ellen Smyth's relationship with Devadas, as she preferred to call him, had developed to treating him as her much-loved son rather than the encumbrance he once had been, and she eagerly anticipated any time they could spend together. Sharing his life had become her life's joy. She wanted to know what he had been doing, what he was studying in class, and what he was thinking, for this was her first foray into maternal love. He was growing up, and she didn't want to miss a moment of this revelation to her heart.

She realized that she must not smother him, so she held the strings loosely. Despite her resolution to share, she spent much of the day thinking about their evenings together, which with his early bedtime was never enough. Hence weekends and the three-week term-breaks became increasingly important.

In the beginning the weekend outings – for that is what they were – were done by The Planes staff. They would take him to the zoo, a favorite, to see a baseball game or other athletic event, or maybe just go for a walk or drive (riding with Simms in his MG-TC was a special treat). As his relationship with Lady Smyth grew, so did her participation in these activities. Gradually, the outings included only Ellen and Devadas. As he became older, Devadas would request the art museum, the natural history museum, or the theater. These activities would usually only take the day. The remainder of the weekend would consist of playing games, watching T.V., and pursuing his hobbies: music and art.

Weekends weren't always just for museums, concerts, and fun. Some were set apart for the learning of useful skills. For example, times were arranged for Devadas to help Fred with his garden and grounds responsibilities. These often involved planting, weeding, trimming shrubs, or working in the greenhouse. Fred said, "Working in the gardens helps you appreciate how much effort is needed to put food on the table, or flowers in a vase." Devadas was quite smug about his gardening skills whenever they ate the vegetables he had grown.

Sometimes, he would help Eliza in the kitchen. She would tell him, "Learning to follow directions is a recipe that will help you be successful in life."

Devadas had his own thoughts on working in the kitchen. One was, "Following a recipe is a lot like playing the piano; it has to be done right to have good results." And another was: "In some ways cooking is like painting because it needs to look right as well as taste right." He thought that cooking or baking was almost as much fun as eating what he had made, but not quite.

The one responsibility that Devadas did not like was cleaning, especially dusting and vacuuming, but he admitted that working with John Hodge enabled them to become good friends.

Working in the shop with Jeb Bedell was off limits until Devadas was older though he sometimes would help with painting. "There are too many ways for a kid to get hurt in the shop. The machines don't care if they whack off a finger or not," said Jeb as he held up his hand with the missing index finger. After Devadas turned twelve, he was occasionally allowed to work with Jeb who gave him advice on using tools safely, "You can never be too careful. After accidents happen, it's too late."

❧

The 'Three Week' learning experiences were different. Although they happened after every ten week term of classes, it seemed that plans were always being made for the next trip. Sometimes, Devadas would make the request, and other times the activity was planned for him. These excursions were rarely repeated.

Some learning experiences were to expose him to different cultures and their languages. Others were for scientific purposes, and all were fun. Hannah or Fred was often called on to accompany Devadas, whereas educational touring companies organized the trips themselves and planned activities and itineraries. But as Ellen and Devadas' relationship grew, Ellen became more and more involved in these excursions as she had in the weekend activities.

One of their best trips was when Ellen took European delivery on a new car, and they traveled without any specific plan or destination, stopping here and there as they were inclined. They enjoyed driving very fast on the autobahns in Germany and leisurely along the byways. Having no schedule provided them with the opportunity to window shop - especially enjoyable at night when the stores were closed but the displays were brightly lit, poking around in bookstores, art galleries, and other places of interest, and eating lunch at street stands or in bakeries. Devadas' fluency in language gave them the advantage of freely mingling with local people, staying at bed and breakfasts and exploring the countryside at their own pace - a treat that was rarely if ever included on a planned itinerary.

⌒

Once, when Devadas was nine years old, Ms. Borhan requested that he accompany her to Madagascar. She said that because she was interested in the behavior of monkeys and apes, she wanted to observe lemurs which are only found on Madagascar and surrounding islands, and she wanted Devad to assist her in her study. Since Lady Smyth had no good reason to refuse her request, Devadas went along.

The flight to Madagascar required flying to Paris and than to Antananarivo, (usually called 'Tana'), the capital. The entire flight required nearly 24 hours, and Ms. Borhan refused to fly first class, preferring coach. After they arrived they took a rickshaw to the hotel. The ride was up and down hills and through hordes of people. By the time they got to the hotel, they were extremely tired, hot and sweaty because it was the rainy season in 'Tana.' Devadas was anxious to get checked in so he could have a shower, change his clothes and get cooled off.

Since the hotel she had chosen was at best second-class with inadequate air-conditioning, Devadas was disappointed and unhappy. Their room was small though it had a window out onto a plaza. He would have preferred to have had his own room but, instead, had to share with Ms. Borhan.

Devadas had no idea where his teacher went every night, nor did he care beyond the normal curiosity of a child. Devadas was an active child who had traveled with the staff and his adopted mother on numerous occasions and could be comfortable in new environments, but not by himself in a second rate hotel room that was neither comfortable nor pleasant.

Ms. Borhan did not like sunlight; she preferred to stay in the hotel room during the day, mostly sleeping. She would go out into the city at dusk, and only once did Devad go with her and then only because he begged to go along. On that occasion they went to a café some distance from the hotel where she met a man with a dark complexion who wore glasses and a Fez.

After ordering a pot of very sweet mint tea which was shared with Devadas, Leily Borhan and the man talked quietly. Because the café was noisy, with some middle-eastern music being played in the background, Devadas was not able to understand the conversation. He believed they were talking Farsi, Ms. Borhan's native tongue, but he wasn't completely sure. He did hear his name mentioned a few times, but that was all. After a while boredom, the noise, and the warm tea lulled him to sleep.

It was very late when Ms. Borhan shook him and said, "Come on, we must go back to the hotel." His joints ached from sleeping in the chair, so he was glad to wake up. He never accompanied her again, nor did he ask.

Devadas was never given the opportunity to explore the city and was, for all intents and purposes, a prisoner in the hotel. They did have television, but the programming was primarily in French and not especially interesting, with a few programs from the B.B.C. and the remainder in Malagasy. Furthermore, the reception was so-so. It is fortunate that he had his drawing materials, for that was his main escape along with the few books he had included in his luggage.

He didn't go hungry, however, for Ms. Borhan always returned with fruit and some kind of 'mofo' or 'koban-dravina,' both sweet fried breads bought from street vendors and not the best diet for a young boy. Since the hotel water was not safe to drink, his choices were fruit drinks, coffee, or tea. It was a real treat when he was allowed a Coke.

One afternoon Leily Borhan left the hotel shortly after lunch and indicated she would be back in the morning. "Now you stay here, watch television, draw, or read. I don't want you to leave the room."

Devadas was normally not disobedient, but he was extremely bored and unhappy and saw Ms. Borhan's early departure as an opportunity to explore. He knew that his teacher had instructed the hotel staff to be sure he stayed in the room, but they had become careless in their acknowledged responsibility, and Devad was able to slip out of his room and through the lobby unnoticed.

He was free and able to explore – at least for a few hours. The Square, upon which the hotel faced was several hundred yards on a side. The street was cobblestone and in the center of the square was a fountain. The square was full of vendors, sights, scents, and sounds. There were many children about his age and size, so he was able to experience this small portion of the city without drawing attention.

He had no money, so buying anything was out of the question. Instead, he watched people as they hurried about. He examined all the items the vendor's were selling and looked at the articles being sold in the shops. Once, when he was examining what appeared to be a flute or whistle of some kind, the shopkeeper chased him away, muttering something in French that sounded like, "You little beggars would steal me blind, if I wasn't watching!"

The church was the most interesting building on the square, clearly the most impressive structure nearby. It was readily visible from their window in the hotel and had bells in one of the two towers. He loved to hear the bells which rang frequently. The church had great wooden doors facing the square, and he was able to open one of the doors and quietly enter the building. Inside, the light was dim, with only a few lights to brighten the interior. Someone was practicing the pipe organ, so he sat on a bench where he wouldn't be noticed and listened to the music.

There were a few people quietly sitting in the pews. Some were just sitting, others had their heads bowed, and some were fingering beads on the necklaces they were wearing. There were two altars at the front where obviously someone would stand and speak. On these were white cloths with gold and purple embroidery. There were many candles.

The building had a certain dignity about it, and the silence and peace therein was in stark contrast to the hurry-scurry outside. The boy lingered in the building for a long time, imprinting the visual images on his mind and the solemnity and tranquility on his soul.

After a time he regrettably returned to the hotel. When he earlier had left the room, he had closed the door which locked behind him. He thought for a moment how to re-enter and, in a wink-of-an-eye, had a plan. He boldly walked up to the desk and spoke to the clerk in French, "Pardon me!"

The clerk looked over the counter and after a moment recognized the boy as the one they were to look after. "What are you doing down here?" he demanded. "Why aren't you in your room?"

Devadas answered, "I stepped out of the room and the door closed, and I need somebody to let me in."

"Oh! Yes! I'll get someone to take you upstairs and open the door. You know you aren't supposed to even step into the hall; it might be dangerous."

His statement could be interpreted, "Do that again, and we may lose a generous tip for keeping an eye on you."

In a moment a boy, not much older than Devadas, came from the office with the key and led him back to his room. When Devadas entered, he breathed a sigh of relief and smiled contentedly about his afternoon.

When they returned to The Planes, Devad was extremely happy to see Ellen Smyth and James Simms waiting with the car at the airport.

Later, when they were alone, Ellen asked Devadas about the trip and what he had learned. Devadas told her of his experiences – at least most of the few that he had – and that he really hadn't done anything but had to remain in their hotel room while Leily Borhan slept.

He said, "It was pretty boring, but I read and made sketches of what I could see from the room's window," which he proceeded to show her. His drawings included the plaza as seen from the hotel with the church being the prominent subject of his pictures. The sketches showed it to be made of some dark gray stone with two flat-topped steeples. On each of the steeples there was a cross and, on the front facing the square, were massive wood doors. Some of Devad's sketches showed people exiting through the doors. Other sketches showed the plaza full of vending stands and people. There were several sketches of the church's interior including one of the altars. Lady Smyth looked at these and wondered if Devadas had told her everything but held her peace.

Ellen Smyth was not happy with Leily Borhan. Her leaving Devadas alone at night without proper supervision and sleeping during the day was simply unacceptable. When she questioned Ms. Borhan about this, Ms. Borhan replied, "My research was on lemurs – and they are nocturnal – and I quickly discovered that being out at night in Antananarivo and environs was not safe for the boy. I paid the night clerk to periodically check on Devad, so I was assured that he was O.K."

Lady Smyth was not happy with Ms. Borhan's explanation and told her that if she wished to have Devadas accompany her on any future trips, she must never let this happen again.

Chapter 6

A Change in the Wind

One beautiful Sunday afternoon Devadas was standing in front of an open window in his room, which was on the second floor, and was intently studying what at first appeared to be a pair of strange dogs that had somehow gotten onto the grounds. As he watched these animals, he remembered a picture of a similar animal in one of his books. He thought for a moment, remembering, and realized that the animals were foxes and, by the color of their coats, red foxes.

He was quite taken by the sight of these two wild animals playing with one another near a number of large whitish rocks grouped in a pile near some pine trees. He didn't want to do anything that might frighten the foxes, but he got the sudden urge to sketch these animals. He quickly and quietly gathered his drawing materials and placed them on the wide, deep windowsill, and, as he opened the sketchbook, he accidentally pushed one of his favorite drawing pencils, causing it to roll toward the edge of the open window.

As he reacted quickly to keep it from rolling off and into the shrubbery below, the foxes heard the noise, perked their ears toward the direction from which the sound had come and instantly disappeared.

"Look what I just did," he said aloud, but to himself. "I scared the foxes away and lost my favorite drawing pencil out the window." And with that he let out a frustrated sigh and dashed from his room to go down below and recover the pencil, if he could find it amidst the shrubs.

As he went to where the pencil would have fallen, he spied a piece of paper that had blown into the bushes and had been caught there by the leaves and branches. Finding litter of any kind on the grounds of The Planes was unheard of and he picked it up, planning to throw it away.

For some unknown reason he decided to look at what he had found. It seemed to have been a page torn from a book of some kind. The paper was very thin, yet strong, and across the top was what appeared to be some kind of title or explanation.

It read – in italics – *"The Passover prepared and the last supper instituted."* At the right it said **St. Luke 21-22**. It was written in two columns.

"I'll look at this later," he thought to himself, and stuffed the scrap in his pocket.

"Now where is my pencil?" and he parted the shrubs with his hands again and again, trying to find it. He had no luck at all until he got down on his knees and peered under the shrubs where he found it sticking straight out of the soil. "It must have fallen straight down and gone right through the bushes point first into the ground below," he thought.

Without another thought he hurried back to his room. As he again looked through the still open window toward the pile of rocks, asked aloud "I wonder if those foxes will ever come back?" He closed the window, gathered his drawing materials, and put them on his desk.

That evening, as he was undressing, he found the scrap of paper in his pocket. Remembering, he straightened it out, threw his dirty trousers on the floor, and sat down at his desk to read what he had found. The format was rather like that of the Koran which Ms. Borhan had him often read.

Reading the words was not difficult, for it was in English but written with "thous, thees, ye's" and unfamiliar words. He had read English like this before, but couldn't remember where. It had to be in class. It reminded him a little of the way Latin was written, as if it had been written a long time ago. It appeared to be a story, or part of one, and since Devadas loved stories, he read all that was there. In the left column, it read:

> For as a snare shall it come on all them that dwell on the face of the whole earth. Watch ye therefore, and pray always that ye may be accounted worthy to escape all these things that shall come to pass, and to stand before the Son of man. And in the day time he was teaching in the temple; and at night he went out and abode in the mount that is call the mount of Olives. And all the people came early in the –

And here the following words were gone, because the rest of the page was torn off.

The right column read:

> thanks, and said, Take this, and divide it among yourselves: For I say unto you, I will not drink of the fruit of the vine, until the kingdom of God shall come. And he took bread, and gave thanks, and brake it, and gave unto them, saying, This is my body which is given for you: this do in remembrance of me. Likewise also the cup after supper, saying, This cup is the new testament in my blood, which is shed for you. But behold, the hand of him that betrayeth me is with me on the table. And truly the Son of man goeth, as –

And that was all.

Turning the scrap over, the left column read:

> And he was reckoned among the transgressors: for the things concerning me have an end. And they said, Lord, behold, here are two swords. And he said unto them, It is enough. And he came out and went, as he was wont, to the mount of Olives; and his disciples followed him. And when he was at the place, he said unto them, Pray that ye enter not into temptation. And he was withdrawn from them about a stone's cast and kneeled down, and prayed, Saying, Father, if thou be willing remove this cup from me: nevertheless not my will, but thine, be done.

And the right column read:

> And after a little while another saw him, and said, Thou art also of them. And Peter said, Man, I am not. And about the space of one hour after another confidently affirmed, saying, Of a truth this fellow was with him: for he is a Galilaean. And Peter said, Man, I know not what thou sayest. And immediately while he yet spake, the cock crew. And the Lord turned, and looked –

And again, the rest of the page was gone.

Devad finished, folded the paper again, and held it in his hands, not moving, but considering what he had just read: the funny English, "a snare," "two swords were enough," "This cup is the new testament in my blood," . . . . . It was a very different story than anything he had read before.

He made a picture; a boy nearly ten years old, young yet mature for his years, sitting at his desk in his shirt and underwear, socks still on, and wearing a look of puzzlement and astonishment, and thinking "What was this that I just read?" Something inside him was stirred, and it was a reaction almost like watching a sunset over the ocean, hearing a bird sing outside his window in the early morning, or seeing the foxes by the rocks – yet it was different.

He couldn't make much sense of what he read. There was only part of a page, and the unfamiliar words and their endings made comprehension difficult; he did not understand the context, although he had seen the word prayer in books that he read. He wasn't at all sure he even grasped that part, and who was this one – "the Son of Man?" praying to? His father?

Devadas finished undressing and, having put on his pajamas, turned out the light and crawled into bed. As he lay there in the dark, his mind wrestled with things beyond his comprehension.

The morning came before he was ready. He awoke to Hannah knocking at his door, saying, "Devad, time to get up. Do you hear me? Breakfast will be ready in thirty minutes. Do you want me to find your clothes?" Devadas obviously mumbled something that sounded like yes, for Hannah opened the door, proceeded to make sure he had a clean towel and washcloth, and laid out his clothes for the day. It was quite dark for the hour, and Devad thought it was probably raining. Before heading for the bathroom, he looked out the window. It was raining. Ms. Borhan would be happy. She didn't like sunshine.

Hannah was done in just a few minutes and left the room with the comment, "Better not dilly-dally. You don't have a lot of time," and Devadas hurried to the bathroom. He thought briefly about the scrap, and what it might mean, then rushed to get finished and down to the staff dining room for breakfast.

When he walked by the kitchen, he smelled the coffee, and bacon and moved quickly to the dining room. When he sat down at the table, Eliza brought in a big plate of pancakes and another of bacon. She had already fixed him a cup of hot cocoa.

As he began to eat, he said, "Eliza! Do you pray?"

Eliza was walking back toward the kitchen but paused and turned. "Where did you come up with that idea?"

He replied in a forced casual tone, "Oh, in something I read. Can you explain it to me?"

Eliza answered hesitantly, "Well . . . . , it is, well . . . , talking to God, like thanking him for your food, or asking him to take care of you while you sleep." Then she added, "When I was a little girl, we always prayed before meals, and my mama prayed with me before I went to sleep."

Devadas continued, "Why don't we pray before we eat?"

Eliza answered guardedly, "When I came to work at The Planes, one of the conditions of the job was that we were never to pray."

Devad looked thoughtful but said no more.

He still had thirty minutes before class, so he put on his raincoat and ran to Fred Riley's cottage. He and Fred were close friends, and, besides, Fred had Taffy, his cocker spaniel. Even though Devad had begged to have a dog, he was not allowed to have a pet of any kind in the Castle, so Taffy was the next best thing.

Before he got to the door, he heard Taffy bark her greeting. Fred opened the door, expecting him, and took his raincoat. Taffy's tail – what there was of it – wagged vigorously, and then she was in Devad's arms as he knelt on the floor.

Devad loved Taffy, but he wanted to ask his friend about prayer, and why praying couldn't be done at The Planes. Standing up, Devad said quickly, "Fred, why don't we pray at The Planes?"

Fred's usual grin, watching Devad with Taffy, faded to a thoughtful furrowed brow, and he rubbed his hand over his blond, brush cut. "Whoa, boy. Where did you come up with that one?"

"I was reading something about someone, I think he was referred to as 'Lord' and 'Son of man,' who was asking his father to have a cup taken from him."

Fred sat down at his kitchen table, let out a large breath of air, and exclaimed, "Aren't you supposed to be with Ms. Borhan at 8:30?"

"Oh yes, I forgot." And as Devad put on his raincoat and stepped out the door to run back to the big house, he said, "But you didn't answer my question." As he dashed away, Fred stood in the doorway, still holding the doorknob with his hand, and shaking his head. "Now what?" he thought.

By the time Devadas was running down the hall toward the classroom area, Ms. Borhan was peering into the hall looking for him. "It's about time you got here young man. You are late, and we have lots to do." With that both went inside, and Devadas slid into his chair.

"Well! I hope you aren't late again. I just don't know what to do with you. If it weren't raining, I would have guessed you were somewhere drawing pictures of trees or something."

~

They were studying Shakespeare. Devadas liked the Bard's work and enjoyed reading and discussing the content. Today the selection was from 'Cymbeline,' one of Shakespeare's comedies, "This is one of my favorite portions," said Ms. Borhan, handing him the book. "Read it aloud to me."

Devadas began to read, but his mind was wandering. Ms Borhan stopped him. "No, no, no!" she said, "You are not getting the rhythm. It is like one of the songs you keep humming when you should be listening. The rhythm goes something like this: 'Ta, ta-da, ta-da, ta, ta-da; ta-da, ta-ta-da, ta-da, ta-da." Devad's artistic sense recognized that even though Ms. Borhan's meter wasn't quite right, he knew exactly what it should be and began again, this time reading with great expression.

FEAR NO MORE THE HEAT O' THE SUN

"Fear no more the heat o' the sun,
    Nor the furious winter's rages;
Thou thy worldly task has done,
    Home art gone, and ta'en thy wages.
Golden lads and girls all must,
As chimney-sweepers, come to dust.
Fear no more the frown o' the great,
    Thou art past the tyrant's stroke,
Care no more to clothe and eat;
    To thee the reed is as the oak,
The scepter, learning, physic, must
All follow this, and come to dust.
Fear no more the lightning-flash,
    Nor the all-dreaded thunder-stone;
Fear not slander, censure rash;
    Thou has finished joy and moan.
All Lovers young, all lovers must
Consign to thee, and come to dust.
No exorciser harm thee!
    Nor no witchcraft charm thee!
Ghost unlaid forbear thee!
    Nothing ill come near thee!
Quiet consumption have;
    And renowned be thy grave!"

And Ms. Borhan smiled in satisfaction.

As Devad was reading, his mind had drifted from the words to the style and similarity of those on the scrap of paper he had found in the shrubbery. "That's it," he thought. "It was written in Elizabethan English." As he paused when done, he decided to ask his teacher what was meant by the title or phrase at the top of the page he had found.

"What is Passover?" he blurted out.

Twice Chosen

"Passover! Whatever does that have to do with Shakespeare? Passover? Where did you come up with that? We've never read or studied anything about Passover." Her reaction was like she had been slapped, and hard at that. She was angry. "Ooh, those damn Jews. I hate them. The world would be better off if they were all dead." Then she caught herself and, with a sickly ingratiating half smile, said determinedly, "I never want to hear you use that word again. Ever!"

Devadas was taken aback. Leily Borhan was not one of Devadas' favorite people, but he admired her teaching ability and her knowledge of literature and language. In all his contact with her, nearly six years, he had never seen her react in this manner. Why did Ms. Borhan hate the Jews, and even want them killed? "I don't understand this."

Later in the week Devadas was passing the kitchen after having eaten lunch with the staff, something he did nearly every day. As he walked by, he called to Eliza, who was working at her desk. As she looked up, she smiled and motioned to him to come in.

"Come here, Devad. I have something you might find interesting." She handed him a brown paper bag. "I shouldn't be giving this to you because of house rules, and I suppose that I might lose my job if Lady Smyth hears about it." And she leaned forward and whispered in his ear, "It's an old Bible."

Devadas looked at her quizzically.

"Bible! You know – Holy Scripture, God's Word. We've had it in our apartment ever since we came here, and we haven't opened it in years – so you can have it. Maybe it will answer your question about prayer."

He thanked Eliza, said that he wouldn't tell anyone, and scampered on down the hall, headed for his room, before going to class. As he ran, he wondered why such secrecy was necessary, and why some words, topics, and objects would be off limits when, from what he had seen, just about anything and everything was O.K. at The Planes.

He tossed the bag with the book on his desk and continued to class. He usually took the stairs because the elevator was out of the way, and, besides, he could run up the steps.

Ms. Borhan was already at her desk when he arrived. She didn't look up, but asked, "What did you have for lunch today? Was it good?"

Devad answered, "Barbecues."

"Pork or beef?"

"I think it was pork."

"Well, I'm glad I ate in my apartment. You know, pork is not clean. The Koran forbids eating it."

The afternoon was spent graphing functions. Devad liked math. It was logical. It had rules. In that way it was like music, for he liked structure –

49

probably why he especially liked rhythms, and harmony, and drawing the details of leaves, flowers, insects etc. So, the afternoon passed quickly.

Because his school day was quite long, and because he was 'the class,' he rarely was given homework or needed it for that matter, and today was no exception. As he opened the door of his room, he looked at his desk and remembered what Eliza had furtively given him.

He sat down and opened the bag. The book was old, but not worn. The cover was leather and said 'bonded cowhide,' whatever that meant, though he guessed he knew. There was nothing written on the title page: no personal data, such as a name. He fingered through the pages from back to front and noted the Bible was organized similarly to the paper found in the bushes below his window. With that he opened his desk drawer where he had put it, brought it out, and compared it to his new acquisition. It only took a few moments to confirm his suspicion that the piece of paper he had found was a torn page from somebody's Bible.

Since he had time before meeting his mother for dinner, he found the book of Luke and began reading it. What he read was like nothing he had ever heard.

"Why?"

He would have to learn more.

Chapter 7

THE HAJJ

It had been three years since the trip to Madagascar, which had not worked out to her satisfaction. Now, Leily Borhan had one more ace up her sleeve. She knew that every ten weeks Devadas' formal education would end, and he would have the three-week break. Usually Ellen Smyth would take him to some city or country where they could be together, and Devadas could broaden his understanding of peoples and cultures, practice his language skills, and add to his worldview.

This time she had asked Lady Smyth if she could take Devadas to Jerusalem to see the Holy City. She would not say that she had planned for the boy to participate in the Hajj, as that might alarm her. Lady Smyth really could not say no, for Ms. Borhan had already obtained the approval of her benefactor, and he thought it an excellent idea and a natural outgrowth of Devadas' studies. By this time Devadas spoke Arabic fluently and would mix well with the myriads traveling to Mecca, a city of nearly two million people located in western Saudi Arabia.

Ellen Smyth grudgingly granted permission for Devadas to accompany Ms. Borhan to Jerusalem. She was not happy about the trip but, with the support and encouragement from the one directing the boy's education, gave her permission. After all Devadas was now twelve years old.

Leily Borhan purchased clothes suitable for the trip. She wanted both Devad and herself to be as inconspicuous as possible, so the clothes chosen were a mixture of western and Middle Eastern. Devad had traveled out of the country many times and already had the necessary passport and travel visas.

Since he was not specifically a Muslim by law, he would be denied entry, but, because he was under the tutelage of Leily Borhan and a minor, he would be granted entry as long as he remained with his teacher.

They would travel by British Air to London and then to Tel Aviv. Their trip from Jerusalem to Mecca would be more difficult. It would take a taxi from East Jerusalem to the King Hussein Bridge and then a JETT bus to Amman. From there they would fly to Mecca. Coming home, it would be quite simple: a direct flight to London and then back to the United States.

Ms. Borhan again insisted they fly tourist class. She said that Devad needed to be with ordinary people rather than those at The Planes, whatever she meant by that. Devad did not enjoy the flight at all. Tourist class was crowded and noisy, and Ms. Borhan seemed to occupy 1-½ seats. She also wore her Jilaabah and headscarf, and that made him uncomfortable. When she spoke to him, it was always in Arabic, like she was trying to make some kind of statement. She also snored when she slept which on the one hand was funny but, on the other, embarrassing. She told him that she always took a pill to help her sleep.

He himself had a hard time sleeping and watching the television was not very interesting. He had a small computer game device, but Devadas really wasn't into computer games. It wasn't that they weren't challenging, but they served no purpose except to amuse, and that aggravated him. He also had his iPod, but he was restless, for whatever reason, and seemed not to be able to concentrate. The food served was adequate but not up to the standards of when they traveled first class.

So, the time passed slowly for the boy.

Heathrow was always interesting. He enjoyed people watching and listening to the languages spoken by the travelers. He kept a log of each language he heard and could distinguish, and how many spoke it. By this time Devadas had mastered French, Spanish, and German, as well as Arabic, and he would now and again make a comment in their native language to watch their reaction to this small boy.

Devadas loved the 'rush' of both take-offs and landings. The activity that accompanied those times had a sense of both danger and urgency. He preferred to be sitting by a window so he could get a sense of speed and location. Unfortunately, on this trip he was one seat in from the aisle, but he had flown enough to have a good idea of what was taking place.

He felt the wheels and flaps go down and the plane slowing. He knew the next thing coming would be the 'thump' of the wheels hitting the runway, the reverse thrust of the engines, and the brakes. Nearly everyone else dreaded these times, but Devad relished them.

Getting their personal gear out of the storage lockers was always a pain. He still wasn't tall enough to help much, so Ms. Borhan had to do it. Everyone was hurrying but then waited for those in front to disembark – it was hurry up and wait. And then they would wait for luggage and go through customs – his least favorite part of traveling by air.

All their papers were in order, so those details were merely a formality. From Ben Gurion Airport Ms. Borhan and Devad took a taxi through West Jerusalem and into East Jerusalem. They were required to again show their visas as they passed through the crossing into East Jerusalem.

Once inside East Jerusalem the taxi took them to their hotel. Devadas noticed the striking difference between West and East Jerusalem. In East Jerusalem the infrastructure was in a state of disarray. It seemed that there was little to no pride in their environment, and the locals seemed to be marked by a sense of hopelessness.

Their hotel was quite adequate and obviously catered to tourists. Once they were settled in their rooms and had a chance to wash away the grime of travel, they went to the hotel dining room for dinner. The dining room was nearly empty, and they sat at a table to themselves and had a light meal of jarjeer salad, chicken fatteh, and cream pudding with pistachios. All was unfamiliar to Devadas, but the cream pudding was especially good.

It was hard for Devadas to go to sleep. First of all, he was again sharing the room with Ms. Borhan, and he was getting to the age where he was no longer a little boy so sharing the room with a woman – especially his teacher Ms. Borhan, – was, well, embarrassing. And then, as on the flight to Israel, she snored. On top of all this, at The Planes he had his own space and the freedom to read, or whatever, without having to share it. And now he had to share the bathroom. He felt hemmed in. Their room was on the third floor and was quiet because it was on more of an alley than a street, so there was little traffic. They had had to carry their bags some distance from where the taxi dropped them off.

Morning came far too soon. Devadas had roused briefly at the morning call to prayer, but Ms. Borhan never heard a thing. The time change worked against them, and they weren't able to wake up until nearly noon. At that time she did her prayers, lamenting her sleeping through the morning Adhan. Devadas had not observed her do her prayers before this trip, so it was somewhat of a novelty for him now.

Ms. Borhan had what was left of the day well planned; they would go to the Al-Aqsa mosque and its 'Dome of the Rock.' Since the hotel was quite close, they would walk. Ms. Borhan told Devad that this was a very sacred place because the dome was built directly over the rock from which Muhammad, escorted by the angel Gabriel, ascended to God in heaven. As an act of worship and respect, they removed their shoes before entering. It was an impressive structure, and Devad was amazed to know that the dome was actually covered by real gold. There was no mention of it being the Jew's Temple Mount or the location where Abraham nearly offered his son Isaac as a sacrifice.

As they walked back toward their hotel, they passed a portion of the old wall, and the Damascus Gate. There were some shops nearby, and Devadas asked his teacher if they couldn't visit some of them. He had decided that he wanted to buy Ellen, his "adopted mother", something that she would like, and so he, too, would remember this trip. One shop specialized in things that were presumably old and supposedly valuable. Devad was not impressed with most of the items. They seemed junky to him, but he did find a painting – a beautiful landscape of a view over the Sea of Galilee toward Tiberius – that he liked and thought was very well done, but the artist was no one he had heard of. He asked the merchant in English what he was asking for the painting.

The merchant thought, "An American child, this should be easy," and he said, "200 dollars."

And because the merchant was probably Palestinian, Devadas replied in Arabic, "200 shekels."

The merchant was taken aback; this he hadn't expected, and he responded again in English, "175 dollars."

Devadas said to the merchant, "You may use Arabic. It is your native tongue, is it not?"

The merchant was not happy dealing with a young boy who obviously knew languages and how to dicker as well. He looked to Ms. Borhan for assistance, but she just smiled as she was very pleased with her student's command of a very difficult language.

The merchant raised both hands in protest and in Arabic said, "400 shekels and not an agorot less."

Devad replied again in Arabic, "300 shekels, and you pack and ship the painting to America."

"All right, all right," answered the merchant. "For you I will do this, but for no one else." And Ms. Borhan paid the merchant and Devadas provided him with the necessary shipping information.

When Ms. Borhan and Devadas awoke, the room was still quite dark. It had been raining, albeit lightly. Israel's climate depends upon the season. Summers are hot and dry, winters are cool and damp – a typical Mediterranean climate - and it was winter.

Breakfast consisted of an almond/date pastry, fresh fruit, and strong coffee. After eating, they took a taxi to the West Bank, where Ms. Borhan wanted Devad to sample Palestinian education and their anger and frustration with the Israeli occupation of their land.

There was a marked contrast between the areas where the Israelis lived and the Palestinians. Israel has built high walls to separate themselves from the Palestinians. When Devadas asked Leily Borhan why these walls had been built and continue to be built, she responded, "The Jews want to take over the entire country for themselves and squeeze the Palestinians into oblivion."

Devadas was not quite able to perceive how the walls would accomplish this. He remembered in his classes when Ms. Borhan had said that in 1948 the newly formed United Nations illegally divided the area now occupied by Israel into two separate states: Israel and Palestine. She said that the Arab world was determined to render this illegal action null and void and attacked the new Jewish nation almost immediately. She said that if the United Kingdom, France and the United States had not been supportive of the new nation of Israel, the Arab consortium would have been successful, destroyed the Jews, and brought peace and prosperity to the area.

Instead, the Jews were successful, three-quarters of a million Arabs fled their homeland, and the refugee situation still festers today. She had further stated that the same thing happened again in 1967, but the Jews were able once again, with help from their allies and the enemies of the Palestinians, to take over even more land.

Confidently, she said that negotiations and continual conflict would accomplish what the wars could never do. She said that the "stupid Jews" would gradually give the Palestinians their land back and, when they became sufficiently weakened, the Arab world would blast them into oblivion. The earth would be better off without the Jews.

"Why did the Jews and Palestinians both claim the same area in the first place?"

When he had asked Ms. Borhan that question, she said that the Jews were all worthless liars and vicious killers.

"They've tried for centuries to take over this area," she had said, "and we have nearly been successful in their annihilation. They have written their own legends, but the Koran provides the only truth about what really has happened. The 12th Imam would one day come and set everything right."

Devadas wondered about these conclusions. There had to be another side to the story.

"If the Jews are as evil as Leily Borhan and the Palestinians believe," he wondered, "why do they still exist, and why weren't all these other nations successful in their hate for the Jews and their planned destruction? And why would they want to come back to the land of their ancestors?"

In Devad's mind there were a lot of unanswered questions.

After a rather rough ride, the taxi let them out by a plain, white, two-storied building with evidence of recent conflict. They were met at the door by the principal or head master of the school. He was dressed in ordinary attire, and, had he been met on the street, he might have seemed a laborer or a merchant. He introduced himself as Ahmad Jabir. He took Devadas to a classroom with nearly 50 students. They all sat in plastic resin lawn chairs, the kind Devad had seen at Wal-Mart or Kmart for under $10.00. All had books, but the only teaching aid used by the teacher was a small chalkboard that students would write upon when called to the front. The only language spoken was Arabic.

Since Devadas was a guest in the school, he was not called on to but only to listen. The class was studying arithmetic. The children were being called to come forward and demonstrate what they knew by doing assigned story problems. Nearly all the problems students were required to do had some aspect of conflict, disobedience, distrust or hate for Israel. A problem presented by a small girl who wore jeans, a pink tee shirt, and white athletic shoes was as follows: "If the country of Israel presently occupies an area of 20,000 square kilometers, has 7,000,000 inhabitants, of which 16% are Palestinian Arabs-

A. How many square kilometers are held by Palestinian Arabs?
B. How may Palestinian Arabs are there in this country?
C. On an average, how much land is held by each Palestinian Arab?

The question was answered successfully by the girl, and then the question was asked:

D. How much of the remaining land is illegally held by the Jews?
E. How much of the land should be owned by Palestinian Arabs?
F. What should happen to the walls?
G. What must happen to all the Jews?

Devadas thought that the math question was appropriate, and he had heard all kinds of denigrating comments about the Jews from Ms. Borhan, but the intensity and passion of the students in the class surprised him. Were not the Jews also entitled to share in the land of their ancestors?

The morning at the primary school passed quickly, and soon the taxi returned to take them back to their hotel. The afternoon would be used in preparing for tomorrow's bus trip to Jordan and the subsequent flight to Mecca. Once there, they would join millions on the annual Hajj to visit the sacred sites and shrines. Leily Borhan explained that the Hajj began earlier than Muhammad and had its origins with Abraham and Ishmael.

Twice Chosen

The bus trip to Amman, Jordan was uneventful and was packed with people traveling to visit relatives, do business and, like them, fly to Mecca.

There was nothing outstanding about the flight from Amman to Jeddah, and the plane was filled with pilgrims, many participating in their first Hajj. Since there were no flights directly to Mecca, all flights land at Jeddah, a very large and modern airport. During a year's time the Jeddah airport serves about 12 million passengers with the largest number arriving for the Hajj. Only once a year at pilgrimage time, a special terminal is used because of the numbers of visitors. It covers about 100 acres and contains its own mosque which can accommodate over 80,000 worshippers at a time.

Ms. Borhan chose to have them travel to Mecca in a taxi, a distance of about 50 miles. Buses frequent that trip, but she decided they would be much more comfortable in the taxi. Because of the Hajj, housing was in very short supply, and Ms. Borhan had planned for that eventuality for months, long before she approached Ellen Smyth about taking Devadas to Jerusalem. They would definitely have a cool and comfortable place to stay until they began their Hajj. With the millions of pilgrims in the city, getting around in Mecca would be a nightmare, so when they did any sightseeing, they would travel on foot. Traffic tie-ups were the norm, and it often took far longer to ride to a destination than to walk.

It was the 8th day of Dha al-Hijjah (Islam's 12th month) – the day of beginning of the Hajj. Ms. Borhan and Devadas were both prepared and in their Ihram dress. Furthermore, they had made arrangements with a vendor for water, food and its preparation. They carried their supplies in backpacks they had brought with them from the States. Ms. Borhan knew that the Hajj could be driven, but she felt it would have much more meaning if done on foot. Besides, the traffic on the four roads from Mecca to Mount Arafat was insane. It would be so much more convenient to be on foot.

As they stepped from their hotel, they were joined by hordes of other pilgrims. Because all were similarly dressed, Ms. Borhan insisted that Devadas take her hand because, if separated, it would be very difficult to find one another. Devadas wasn't at all happy with this arrangement but recognized the logic of her request.

The heat hit them, and it wasn't summer. There were no clouds in the sky. It was intensely blue, and because of the absence of clouds the sun seemed unusually bright. The buildings, almost exclusively white, reflected the sun's radiation. It was fortunate they were using sunscreen and had umbrellas. They also carried water, for dehydration was a great threat and thousands would suffer from heat problems doing the Hajj.

Devad was not happy. Not only was he uncomfortable due to the heat and the clothing he wore, he could not see anything due to the quantities of people, and the smell of human bodies was almost over powering.

They moved at the rate of the crowds engulfing them. For Ms. Borhan this was absolute delight. For Devadas it was hell. He wondered how anything like this would lead to anything but frustration and disillusionment. It had to be one's frame of mind.

The first rite to be performed was the first Tawaf, or the seven trips (counterclockwise) around the Kaabah. The Kaabah was the most sacred site of Islam. Its origin was lost in antiquity, but evidence existed that it had been a sacred site of Arabian tribal gods, and that Muhammad rededicated it to Allah. The eastern cornerstone of the Kaabah was the 'Black Stone,' the ancient sacred stone that, according to tradition, dated back to the time of Adam and Eve. It was mounted in a silver frame, and the lower part of the border was studded with silver spikes. Supposedly, when it fell from heaven, it was white in color and became black because of the sins of mankind.

On each pass around the Kaabah, each pilgrim tried to get close enough to be able to kiss the Black Stone. Because of the huge number of people, most could not get close enough to the Black Stone to kiss it, but were merely able only to point toward it.

On the sixth circuit around the Kaabah, they were able to get close enough for Ms. Borhan to kiss the stone, but Devadas would not. But, as he passed close, it appeared as if the Black Stone was supported by the nails in the silver frame, and, as his gaze was held for that brief moment, he heard words in English in his mind, "These pierced my hands and my feet." He shook his head.

"It must be the heat and the crowds," he thought. But because of the crowding of those behind him, he had little time to consider this unusual thought.

When the seventh trip was completed, they moved on to the second activity, the observation of Hagar's search for water for her son who was dying of thirst. There were two adjacent hills between which Hagar traditionally searched to find water. In his frustration and impatience, Ishmael is said to have stamped his foot, and Allah brought about a spring, now called the well Zamzam. Seven trips between the hills were required before they would drink from the well.

There were large tents set up on the Plains of Mina, which was about midway between Mount Arafat and Mecca. There, Devadas and Ms. Leily Borhan rested with the other pilgrims. The tents were huge and white, to reflect the light, and held thousands.

Twice Chosen

In the morning after a breakfast of fruit, pastries, and bottled water, they proceeded on to Mount Arafat. It was here that Muhammad preached his last sermon and, in remembrance of that event, they quietly and contemplatively stood from mid-afternoon until sunset, quietly praying and considering the course of their lives. This was the most difficult time for Devad, for he was an active boy, and standing there with thousands of people in a defined area was very difficult. At times he would try to sit down, but Ms. Borhan would quickly raise him back to his feet. Hot, boring and uncomfortable – but it was to change – a little.

In the cool of the evening, the pilgrims moved almost in mass to Muzdalifah, which lay between Mina and Mount Arafat. There each would collect 49 pebbles or stones for the next day's ritual of stoning the Devil. This was something a young boy could enjoy, for rock collecting, whatever the reason, was always fun. The only problem was the number of people picking up the pebbles. The difference between most of the Hajj participants and Devadas was that others picked up their collection for throwing, while he picked up the pebbles for their appearance or content. In science they had done enough geology for the boy to recognize some of what he found. Many of the pebbles appeared to be made of granite of some kind, and most were rounded which, as he remembered was due to being carried along by water though that was hard to believe with the extent of desert all around him. If there ever was water there, it had been a long time ago.

On day three, they stayed in Mina and threw the stones at the three concrete pillars, really short walls, walls that represented the Devil. Abraham was believed to have been tempted by the Devil three times, and each time he refused, hence the three stonings.

They were to hit each pillar 7 times. Devadas enjoyed this exercise, though with the pillars as big as they were, it really wasn't much of a challenge. The stones were thrown from the multi-leveled Jamarat Bridge which was built to accommodate the large number of people throwing the stones.

Because Ishmael was to be sacrificed, and Allah supplied a ram as a substitute for Abraham's faithfulness, following the stoning of the Devil each pilgrim was to similarly sacrifice a sheep. Because of the huge number of people this was impossible, so many used a voucher to have a sheep slaughtered in their name. With millions of sheep sacrificed, there was too much to be eaten by each worshipper, so the excess was packaged and shipped around the world to feed the poor.

On the fourth day, they again performed the Tawaf at Masjid Al Haram, the mosque in Mecca, with a repeat of the seven circuits around the Kaabah, and then returned to Mina to again throw stones at the pillars representing the Devil.

On day five, they returned to Mecca where they did their third Tawaf. After they had finished, Devadas asked to return and again throw stones at the Devil. Ms. Borhan consented.

And their Hajj was completed. Upon their return to the hotel, the air-conditioning, their showers and a change in clothes was a great relief. Devad was so thankful that it was over. It was difficult for him to comprehend how many people from so many countries were there for their pilgrimage. For him the Hajj held little meaning, though he recognized that it had deep religious significance for many, but everything seemed so cut and dried – almost like a religious theme park. The highlight for Devadas was the picking up the pebbles and throwing them at the pillars. But there was the time he thought he heard the Black Stone speak to him. What was it that he thought he heard? "These pierced my hands and my feet." Whatever did that mean? Weren't Jesus hands and feet pierced by nails? Could God have been using the Black Stone and the Hajj to remind him of the true provision for mankind?

Chapter 8

CONCLUSIONS

The trip back home was tiresome and tedious. The only advantage was that the jet lag was not nearly as troublesome as their trip east.

Ellen Smyth had James drive her to the airport to meet the travelers. Ms. Borhan, though tired, was euphoric about the trip, while Devad was ecstatic to be home to familiar surroundings: his music, his art, the banter with the staff, his own bed, and the evening meals with his adopted mother.

Lady Smyth was overjoyed to see Devadas, for she had missed him so very much. The time had truly dragged, and dinnertime was the worst part of the day.

It was mid-evening when they got back to the estate. Ms. Borhan quickly excused herself and hurried off to her room. Devad felt both tired and dirty, but he wanted to spend time with his mother, so while Hodge carried his luggage to his room, Devad and Ellen Smyth slipped into the staff dining room, something she almost never did, so Devad could have a glass of milk and some of his favorite cookies.

"Tell me about your trip," prompted Lady Smyth.

"It was pretty boring," replied Devad.

"Well, tell me where you went and what you did," was her response.

"We went to Jerusalem, but we didn't go to the new part except to drive through. Instead, we went to the old part. My favorite was seeing the Dome of the Rock. I did buy you a present. Did you get it?"

"Not yet," Ellen Smyth replied.

"Oh!" Devadas was obviously disappointed.

"Well, what did you get me?" asked Ellen.

"It is a painting of the Sea of Galilee. I thought it was really well done."

"Sometimes it takes weeks for something like that to arrive," said Ellen. "It will come. You have to be patient. What else did you do?"

"We went into what was called the West Bank. Do you know that they have nearly completed a high wall between the Jewish part of Israel and the Palestinian?" said Devad.

"Why?" asked Ellen.

"Those people hate each other," said Devad in reply, as he munched on one of his cookies.

"I've seen a lot about their conflict on television and in the newspapers, but I really don't understand their deep-seated hatred for each other. I think the wall was built to prevent terrorists from carrying bombs and blowing themselves up in the public areas in the Jewish sectors," said Ellen thoughtfully, "I'm glad you weren't exposed to such horror."

"Ms. Borhan took me to one of the Palestinian schools to observe. It was really different being one of fifty or so children rather than being the only one in the class. I rather enjoyed being with the other kids."

"Where was Ms. Borhan while you were in the class?"

"She was talking to the person she referred to as the head master."

"Hm. You were gone for a little longer than two weeks. What else did you see?"

Devadas knew that his adopted mother didn't know about the Hajj, and he was a little reluctant to talk about that because he didn't know what her reaction might be. But after a slight pause, he answered, "We went to Mecca."

"Mecca!" Ellen Smyth exclaimed, "Why Mecca?"

"Because Mecca is where Muslims go for their pilgrimage."

"But isn't Mecca out in the middle of nowhere?" asked his mother.

"Mecca, at least what we saw of it, is a very modern city with nearly two million inhabitants, and because of the Hajj – "

"What do you mean Hajj?" interrupted Ellen Smyth.

"The Hajj is the Muslim pilgrimage. One thing they do during the Hajj is march seven times around a cubic stone shrine in a huge mosque. At one of the corners of the cubic building is a Black Stone mounted in a silver frame. Everyone is supposed to kiss the Black Stone. I didn't, but it I think it talked to me. Did you ever have anything like that happen? I don't think it said anything to anyone else."

Ellen Smyth screwed up her face in a thoughtful way, and replied, "Maybe! What did it say?"

"It said, 'These pierced my hands and my feet.' What would that mean?"

"What was it that pierced somebody's hands and feet?"

"I don't know. There were a series of silver nails that seemed to hold up the Black Stone. Maybe it was talking about them." And Devadas was quiet for a moment, revisiting that moment and his tentative conclusion.

He continued, "My favorite part was picking up stones and throwing them at the Devil, oh, not really the Devil, but at three walls. We threw the stones from a bridge that had several levels."

"Why did the bridge have several levels?"

Devad replied, "I'm not completely sure, but I think it is because thousands of people were throwing stones at the same time."

"Well! Did you enjoy yourself?" asked his mother.

"Not really. It was hot, crowded, boring, and I had to hold onto Ms. Borhan's hand so we wouldn't get separated. There were too many people, we got pushed and shoved, I couldn't see very much, and lots of people smelled bad. I'm glad to be home."

"Well, I'm glad you are home too," and she decided then and there that she would never let Devad go again with Leily Borhan, even if she did have it cleared with that one who had brought her son to her.

༄

The scrap of paper in the shrubbery, the prohibition of prayer and the Bible, the Muslim's irrational hatred of the Jews, the words heard while near the Black Stone – all prompted Devadas to do some research in the Bible about Abraham, Isaac, and Ishmael. So he began to read Genesis, the book of beginnings. As Devadas read about the life of Abraham, his eyes grew wide. While on the Hajj, a sheep was sacrificed in honor of Ishmael who was reputed to be the one Abraham was to sacrifice, but the Bible said that Isaac was the one placed on the altar. Hagar was Sarah's Egyptian handmaid, and Ishmael was her son. Isaac was the long awaited and promised son of Abraham and his wife Sarah. Which would be the ultimate sacrifice for the testing of Abraham's faith? Would it not be Isaac? It would seem that the Hajj tribute to Abraham, Hagar and their son Ishmael was misplaced. It should be to Abraham, Sarah, and the miracle son, Isaac.

This conclusion of Devadas was momentous. If he was correct, and he had every reason to believe that he was, the consequences were:

#1. The Koran cannot be regarded as 100% reliable.

#2. If it is in error on one point, didn't that cast doubt on the remainder?

#3. Events such as the Hajj have no special spiritual value, for the people are deluded.

Devadas was sure that he must talk with Ms. Borhan. She was so devout in her faith and her hatred for the Jews so intense, how she would react to his logic? While he wanted to clear this up, he was sure she would again become angry, and that made him afraid. How should he present his conclusions? He decided that he would write everything down, so there would be no mistakes made by misunderstanding what he said.

It would have been quite easy for Devadas to have written his thesis, had he a computer, but Leily Borhan did not like computers and would not allow them. She did not even want Devadas to have access to a computer because computers might divert his attention, which she reasoned would negatively impact what she wanted him to learn.

So, Devadas proceeded to handwrite his conclusions and their explanations. Devadas' mind was far advanced, but he was still a young boy, and his writing skills lagged well behind his thinking, so his efforts lasted late into the night. He sat at his desk and used only the desk lamp. In addition he put one of his bath towels on the floor to block out any light that might be seen under the door, for what he was doing was much too important to have Hannah, Mary, or his mother checking up on him and telling him to go to sleep.

When he went to class the next morning, it was again a rather dark and dismal day, and Ms. Borhan was in a jovial mood. She even greeted him with a smile rather than her usual glare. She noticed that he had a folder filled with something, so she said, "I don't remember giving you any assignments. What do you have in the folder, some of your art work or maybe something to read when you are supposed to be listening to me?"

"Sit down, Devadas. Let me look at what you have." Devadas timidly handed her the folder with his conclusions and their reasons and remained standing in case he would need to make a hasty exit. As Ms. Borhan read, she began to scowl. Her expression became black. Then she did the most curious thing. As she continued reading, she began to cry. When she finally looked up, her eyes were red, and her cheeks were wet with tears.

Finally she spoke. "After all I have done for you, and this is the way you treat me. Why? I've taught you nearly everything I know. I've taken you to the holy city. I've shared my meals with you. I have never told you anything that isn't true, and yet you scorn me. You tell me I am a liar. May Allah punish you in the fires of Hell forever."

With that she rose from her chair and quietly left the room. Devadas never expected this reaction. He didn't know what to make of it. He expected to her to become angry and dispute his thinking, but this? Why didn't she try to correct and show him where he was wrong, if that was the case. This turn of events convinced him that he was right, and what he said had struck much too close to home.

Devadas stayed in the classroom area, waiting for Leily Borhan to return. When she didn't, he grew increasingly uncertain what to do. Finally, he left the classroom area and went downstairs to see if she had gone to get help to discipline him, but that didn't make sense either. Discipline him for what? All he had done had been in the realm of ideas. He hadn't been bad or disrespectful.

His first stop was in the office. Elizabeth was at her desk, working at her computer. As Devadas entered, she looked up and said, "Devad! Aren't you supposed to be in class? What are you doing down here?"

Devadas responded, "Have you seen Ms. Borhan? I showed her something I had written, and she started to cry and walked out. I don't know where she went."

Elizabeth looked puzzled. "That is odd. Let me check with the others and see if they have seen her." And with that she did an all-stations page and asked if anyone had seen Ms. Borhan.

The responses were all negative, and it was only seconds until Ellen Smyth entered the office, wondering what was happening. Devad was relieved to see her and quickly related the concern.

Lady Smyth summoned Hannah, Mary, and Hodge to the office and asked them if they would help her find Ms. Borhan, for she had disappeared quite suddenly and inexplicably. She wanted to find out where she had gone and get her explanation.

Hannah and Mary went upstairs to the classroom area. Ms. Borhan had not returned, nowhere to be seen, and, by the look of her desk, she had never been there – it showed no evidence that it had ever been used. Lady Smyth, Hodge, and Elizabeth went to her quarters on the fourth floor. The door of her apartment was open, and, like the classroom area, there was no evidence that she had even been in the room. She was gone.

Upon their return to the first floor, they assembled all the staff and asked if anyone had seen Leily Borhan. None had. The conclusion was that she must have left the premises, although this was not as simple as it might seem. The gates at the main entrance and the service entrance were kept closed. Anyone visiting The Planes could leave at any time, for the gates and fencing were not built to keep people in, but rather to keep the unwanted out. Computers and surveillance cameras monitored opening and closing of the gates, and records of those entering and leaving were available.

This information required some time to retrieve, so Lady Smyth had Elizabeth check her records to determine if Ms. Borhan had let herself out of either gate. The day's records revealed no one leaving or entering except for the food service company's daily delivery. A call to them indicated that they had seen nothing unusual, nor did any additional people come in or go out with them.

"She failed in many ways. She failed to gain the boy's confidence, and, even though she taught him how to learn and process information, she made no headway in directing his thought processes. Instead of at least acknowledging his interest in music or art and shaping his tastes toward our purposes, she fought him, and his resolve was strengthened."

Another voice chimed in, "And somehow she allowed a piece of the accursed 'light' to penetrate the boy' mind."

"And revealed her attitude toward the scum of all people," said another.

"Her reclusive behavior alienated her from Lady Smyth and her staff," said a third.

"And you are all correct in your understanding," said the chief adversary. "This time we shall succeed. The one I've picked to replace Leily Borhan doesn't realize he is in my pocket, but his intellect is strongly skewed in our direction, and his distaste for anything that has the possibility of a connection to 'Him' is exactly what we want. The boy has great intellect. We will appeal to his pride and maneuver and shape him to believe that his ability to reason is enough, and nothing or no one else is necessary. When we accomplish that, he is ours forever."

Chapter 9

TRY AGAIN

The brief vacation from his schooling was short lived. Ellen Smyth was once again contacted and told that the new tutor would be coming to The Planes, a young man named Kris Gustafson. No mention was made of Ms. Borhan or of her sudden and unexplained departure. Mr. Gustafson would be arriving the next day. He had his own car so would bring himself to The Planes.

When Kris Gustafson arrived at the and identified himself, Elizabeth remotely opened it and instructed him to come to the front entrance and to leave his car parked in one of the spaces provided. She said that Hodge would meet him at the door and show him into the drawing room where Lady Smyth would meet him.

First impressions are important, and when Dr. Gustafson was shown into the drawing room, Hodge requested he sit down, told him that Lady Smyth would be with him in a moment, and asked him if he would like something to drink.

In a very brief time, Mary brought him his coffee, and he sat pondering his new job and what it might entail. When Lady Smyth entered the room, Kris rose and introduced himself. Ellen Smyth was impressed at the new teacher's manners and the way he presented himself. And Kris Gustafson was equally impressed with the surroundings and Lady Smyth's cordial welcome and handshake.

After the introductions and other formalities, Kris Gustafson asked if he could see where he would be teaching and staying. Ellen Smyth was quite proud of the classroom area, personally led Dr. Gustafson to the elevator, and took him to the third floor where he would be teaching Devadas.

When he entered the area, he gasped, "This is beautiful," and proceeded to examine almost every detail. As he looked at the excellent materials and tools provided, he could be heard saying, "Incredible! Good choice!" and other superlatives. After his exploration, he turned to Lady Smyth and said, "I've never been in a better facility then this. You are to be complemented for what you've done."

"Thank you! It was somewhat of a miracle that we were able to do this and with such short notice as we were given."

"At that Kris Gustafson looked at her curiously and said, "I'd like to hear that story someday. However you did this, it is truly remarkable."

Then he asked, "May I see where I will be staying?"

"Certainly! It is just down the hall." And she took him to where she and Devadas had decided he should stay.

When Lady Smyth opened the door, he saw a spacious three-room apartment.

"Why, this is great. I will have room for my books and sound system. And it is close to where I will be teaching."

Lady Ellen Smyth smiled slightly and replied, "I'm glad you like it. I'll have Hodge help you with your luggage, and show you where you will leave your car."

～

Other than his excellent academic credentials, the new teacher was very unlike Leily Borhan. He was a very ordinary-appearing person. At first acquaintance he gave the impression of being quiet and retiring, but that was quite misleading. He was extremely self-confident and would discuss most subjects with an air of superiority that at times made conversation difficult. His favorite phrase was, "Well, the point is," spoken with a nearly imperceptible rise of the chin, his eyes slightly narrowed and with a slight pause to allow the listener to grasp the full significance of his intellect.

Within the first few days at The Planes, he suggested ways that nearly every operation in the manse could be improved, from how Eliza should make gravy, how shrub trimming could be improved, to why the office electronics should be replaced. He made himself available to anyone and everyone when not in the classroom or working on his computer, and it took less than 48 hours for the staff to make themselves scarce when they saw him coming.

At least Devad did not find him intimidating, as was the case with Ms. Borhan. Devadas liked his new teacher and was impressed with his confidence and intelligence. In turn, he liked Devadas and made it his goal to expand his knowledge and develop his intellect.

He soon had Devadas using the computer, and the boy was quickly at ease with all its intricacies. The computer instantly became his window into the "everything" of his curiosity. He was very careful to allow adequate time for music and art, as well as his studies. Sometimes, however, rather than answering Devadas' questions, the computer sometimes led him to further question what he read and saw, causing him to look at the world in unconventional ways.

In many ways, Kris Gustafson seemed over-prepared to be the sole teacher of a boy as young as Devadas, even with his great intellect. Kris had a B.S. in biology, an M.S. in biophysics, and his Ph.D. in the history of science, all from prestigious universities.

Because of his interests and training, the new teacher no longer emphasized the classics, but purposefully directed his teaching toward the sciences and their interaction with philosophy. He had been selected precisely because of this perspective. While he was unaware, the furtive plan was to capitalize on Devad's amazing intellect, hoping one day to shape the future for ulterior purposes.

Kris Gustafson soon had Devadas reading his favorite thinkers, such as Hume, Rousseau, Darwin, Huxley, Futuyma, Crick, Dawkins, Gould, and others of similar ilk. Gustafson had no patience with the non-rational thinking of the day. Postmodernism to him was as abhorrent as was any other 'religious' point of view, for he was a staunch believer in naturalism. He pushed the idea that man was but a part of the great circle of life and had achieved more because he had evolved an optimum set of tools with which to work. Therefore, man was able to dominate all the other forms of life yet was at the same time indebted to them.

∽

"Nature has given you great intellect," he said one day to Devadas. "Because of your intellect, you have been given a mission to humanity. You have in you the ability to change the course of history, to alter the world and shape it for the good of man.

How old are you, Devad?"

"Twelve," the boy responded.

"Exactly," said Mr. Gustafson, "and how old is the country of the United States?"

Devad paused as he considered this and then answered, "Something a bit over 200 years."

"Again you are right. And the Enlightenment is approximately – "

"Three hundred years old," concluded Devadas.
"Again you are right. Now when did the Industrial Revolution begin?"
"Somewhere around 1800, but it was after the Enlightenment."
"Exactly," replied his teacher, " And do you think there is any connection?"
Devadas looked thoughtful. "It would seem so. The Industrial Revolution certainly followed the Enlightenment."
"And what was the Enlightenment?"
"That reason was the ultimate source and basis of authority."
"And what was the source and basis for authority before reason?"
"The church, religion, and superstition probably," said Devadas.
"Again you've nailed it," said his teacher. "And consequently, there seems to be a strong connection between the Enlightenment and the Industrial Revolution. You see, the application of reason, as opposed to dogma, irrationality and the like, ushered in a great revolution, not only in invention and manufacturing, but also in the political, legal, economic and philosophical realms. We would likely still be locked into the illogical dark ages were it not for reason replacing dogma. Sadly, nature has been left to fend for itself, because of man's carelessness or indifference, but that is a topic for the future."
Devadas recognized some truth to the position his teacher was presenting but felt it was an oversimplification. For a twelve year old, he had already seen and learned much, and he stubbornly refused to jump to conclusions until he could consider all the information available and extrapolate the idea or ideas to their logical conclusions.
Kris Gustafson continued, "Let me take this reality a bit farther, by asking you some more questions. In the last two hundred or so years, what has happened to information? No, don't answer me yet, but since the Industrial Revolution has occurred, how has the world changed?"
Devadas could see where this was going but answered, "Oh, there have been incredible changes in the development of power, transportation, medicine, the transmission of information, with, of course, the recent development of electronics, radar, television, computers, cell phones etc."
"That's my point. Our standard of living is what it is because superstition and dogma have been replaced by the scientific approach and not wasting time with details that can't be verified or tested in a laboratory. Our great strides are the product of freeing the mind from religious dogma and superstition. Do you have any questions?"
"Well," answered Devadas. "religion and faith play a great part in the lives of most of the world's inhabitants. While on the Hajj, I saw millions from all over the world who were there because of their beliefs."

"And how is their lifestyle?" countered his teacher.

"The cities are very modern, and their lifestyle is not so very different from ours."

"You said you were in the West Bank. What was the situation there?"

"It wasn't good. But they blamed it on being repressed by the Jews."

"And that, too, is a product of religious dogma, isn't it?"

"I guess it is," Devadas acquiesced.

At this Kris Gustafson leaned back in his chair and smiled. "The superiority of the mind over emotion, of reason over dogma, has resulted for the Western world in a higher standard of living, more leisure time, increased longevity, and a host of other benefits never before seen by man."

He continued, "O.K., let's take a trip through time, back to the beginning, and see how reason and the mind unlock the myriad secrets of creation. How old is the earth, Devad?"

"From my reading I think the earth is nearly 5 billion years old."

"Right! The best figure that we have for the age of the earth is a wee bit more than 4.5 billion years. This figure is based upon evidence gathered from several sources – mostly from asteroids or meteorites, and rocks brought back to the earth from the moon which have been dated by radioactive age dating – in this case Uranium 235, Uranium 238, and their ultimate decay products, often called daughter products, which are stable or non-radioactive. We assume that the earth, which has undergone extensive weathering and plate tectonics, was formed simultaneously with the rest of the solar system. Thus the age of meteorites should provide an accurate age for the earth.

"Now, what about the age of the universe?"

"From what I've read, about three times older than the solar system," speculated Devadas.

"That is about right. Do you know what the age of the universe is based upon?"

"No," said Devad, "What?"

"The predominant methods are #1, the evolution of globular clusters, and #2, the rates of recession of stars and galaxies."

"Please explain what both of these mean. I'm not sure I understand."

"Rates of recession of stars and galaxies is relatively straight forward and points to the concept of the 'Big Bang.'"

"Stars and groups of stars or galaxies emit light. The light travels from these sources to where we live on earth. Light carries information. The light emitted by a star passes through its envelope of cooler gases because each star will have a slightly different composition. Each element present in that envelope of gases absorbs certain specific wavelengths of light, resulting in what is known as an absorption spectrum, appearing as dark lines at specific wavelengths where the light has been absorbed by the elements present. We are able to measure the distances between these lines with great accuracy. Each particular element has its own spectrum or the spaces between the lines when that gas absorbs the light given off by a stationary object.

An object moving away from the observer will have all the lines slightly farther apart - a longer wavelength, and an object moving toward the observer will have all the lines slightly closer together. This change in spacing is proportional to the speed of the object emitting the light relative to the position of the observer. As you probably know, blue light has shorter wavelengths, and red light has longer wavelengths. The starlight from the stars we observe is shifted toward the red, thus they are becoming farther away. If you extrapolate the change in their velocities, you can calculate when they were located at a single point. Since our measurements are continually being refined, the consequent age of the earth is constantly becoming more accurate, but there are many other factors that become involved. For instance, if the universe is expanding, that expansion also moves stars and galaxies farther apart."

Devadas had no trouble following the development but asked, "What about the evolution of globular clusters?"

Mr. Gustafson replied, "That is beyond my area of expertise. I can't answer that one."

"This has been a good discussion, but I want to turn it in another direction. First, let's take a break. I'd like to get a cup of coffee. Let's go down to the kitchen to see what we can find. I'll bet you could get some milk or cocoa. Maybe there will be some cookies or donuts or something to help soak up our drinks." And out they went. Devadas had been sitting for a long time, and he, too, was ready to get up and move around.

The kitchen staff was working on both lunch and dinner, but they loved having Devadas around and never begrudged giving him a snack. Having Kris Gustafson come too, was very different from when Ms. Borhan was at The Planes. She rarely took her meals with the staff and certainly never took breaks. Nobody knew what she did for food. She must have prepared her meals in her apartment.

After Kris had finished his coffee, he headed upstairs, but Devadas took a minute to see if his adopted mother was in her office. Elizabeth looked up from her desk as Devad came in. "Hi kiddo! How are you and your new teacher getting along?"

"I like him. He's interesting and fun, and the things we're studying are more interesting too."

At that moment Ellen Smyth stepped out of her office: "What are you doing here? Aren't you supposed to be in class?"

"We took a break. I just wanted to say hi!"

"Well, I'm glad you came in. I've tickets to the opera on Sunday. I think it is one you will like, 'The Magic Flute.'"

"Great. I love Mozart. Thanks, Mother, I'll see you at dinner time." And with that Devadas was off to class, anxious to hear where his teacher would take their discussion regarding the age of the earth.

"Our quest is to determine where life began and how. Review for a minute. The Universe is something like 15 billion years old, and the earth and solar system are about 4.5 billion year old. We are unable to visit the vast reaches of the past, but we can make some basic assumptions that will enable us to fill in the gaps or our lack of observation.

The first assumption is what some refer to as 'Uniformitarianism.' This makes a lot of sense because we conclude that the processes shaping the earth today shaped the earth in the past. I will modify it somewhat by saying the chemical and physical processes acting today are those that have acted since the beginning, not saying anything about their intensity or rate. When the Big Bang occurred, which we refer to as a 'singularity,' or when all conditions were essentially infinite, our assumptions about chemical and physical processes don't apply, for all conditions – temperatures and pressures – at that time exceeded anything measurable or imaginable."

"We make the assumption that life originated on the earth, but an alternative position is that life could have developed elsewhere in the universe and been transported via a comet, meteorite, or by some other mechanism. Life exists, that's a given. The earliest record of life on earth is about 3.5 billion years ago. What caused life, even simple unicellular life, remains unknown - at least at this time.

If there hasn't been enough time for it to be formed on earth, there certainly has been enough time since the beginning of the Universe. Energy would definitely be required, because structure derived from randomness cannot happen without the application of energy. The possibilities for supplying such energy are nearly endless. Electrical energy from electrical discharge such as lightening, heat energy from heat flow emanating from the earth's interior, nuclear energy from early concentration of radioactive materials are all possibilities, and there may have been several sources working in concert. But it did happen."

Devad was bouncing up and down with the urge to ask a question.

"O.K. Devad, what do you want to say?"

"What about creation? Couldn't there be some kind of higher intelligence that created life. On the Hajj there were thousands, maybe millions, who believed that God was responsible for life. I know that because they believe that God is alive and real. They pray five times a day and spend much time and money to do the Hajj."

"All right, Devad, design an experiment that would prove the existence of God. Science excludes God or gods because they are not scientifically testable. Creation is an untenable explanation for life because a god cannot be proved and cannot be measured. The entire concept of god as an explanation was appealing when science had not developed sufficiently to provide and alternative solution. Evolution is that mechanism that can describe scientifically the origin of 'first life.'"

This was not a convincing argument, because already in his short life there were events that were beyond the realm of science, that pointed strongly towards someone or something outside the box of things measurable and testable, but for the time being, he would wait and think about it.

These thoughts were interrupted as his teacher continued. "One thing is certain. Once life began, however it happened – and one day we will know – life spread very quickly and evolved with ever more complex forms spreading across the entire planet. The pattern seems to be one from simple to complex, from the sea to land, the latter being a somewhat convincing argument that the original life formed in the seas with increasing diversity and complexity. Thus, single celled organisms evolved to multi-celled, and that occurred very early after the earth was formed."

"Mr. Gustafson, explain what you mean by evolution. Evolution is a term that is often used in my books, but I need to know what you mean when you use the word."

Kris Gustafson obliged Devadas, and said: "Evolution is the gradual but continuous genetic adaptation of organisms or species to their environment resulting in forms that differ significantly from their beginnings. An example or two should help. Reptiles are believed to have evolved from fish, and mammals from reptiles. There are many unanswered questions because so many details remain lost in the ancient past. Basically, all we have had to go on has been the fossil record, but recent developments in the study of DNA reveal similar DNA sequences in the genome of most organisms which seems to indicate common ancestry."

Devadas interjected, "If evolution has been a gradual but continuous change, shouldn't there be a lot of evidence of failed change? DNA sequencing may show similarities, but the fossil record, even if it is incomplete, should show transitions."

"Yes it should, but truth be known, those connections are nearly all missing. It seems that a species exists for a prolonged period of time, and then, suddenly, there appears a new species apparently derived from the first but in addition to the original. The time of such a change is very short in terms of the geologic record, nearly instantaneous, hence leaving little chance of a record. This abrupt change has been termed, 'punctuated equilibrium.' There seems to be no explanation for that, other than the change occurs. I am certain that someday we will understand that process."

Devadas grasped the idea that life originated somewhere on the earth's surface many millions of years ago as a chance reaction of molecules somehow combining in some high energy environment, but was vaguely troubled. If it happened in the long ago past, why was it not occurring at the present. After all, similar conditions were known to exist at present in areas such as Yellowstone National Park and at the vents marking the axes of the mid-ocean ridges, and where was the evidence?

He was also puzzled by the incredible variety of life and why it should increase in complexity even if solar and other forms of energy were available. Mere chance seemed quite improbable as the explanation.

That Devadas liked and admired Kris Gustafson provided some impetus to accept his teacher's ideas, but he needed time to think through what he had been told and the ramifications. He wanted to settle these ideas, for there were only two alternatives – creation or chance – and faith was required for either choice. So, resolution had to be somewhere other than the realm of science.

∽

Devad's preoccupation with origins caused him to interrogate his teacher unmercifully about these ideas. His questions became increasingly sophisticated, and perceptive. Usually these question and answer periods would come to an end by his teacher throwing up his hands and giving the stock adult/child answer, "Because! That's why! As you study and get older, you will understand." Kris would leave the classroom area on those days shaking his head. It had always made sense to him when he was a student both in high school, and the university, so why couldn't Devadas understand?

He knew that Devadas' mind was far more competent and agile than his, to his chagrin, for he pictured himself as quite intellectual. Often, upon return to his apartment in the evenings, he would spend hours wrestling with these questions, sometimes reading and taking notes far into the night. He, on occasion, called his thesis professor for assistance.

Devadas Smyth never phrased his questions in a manner to put down his teacher, (that is an adult thing), but to satisfy his unquenchable thirst to know. Kris Gustafson recognized this and did his best to assist Devadas in his quest. Kris's presentation had one fatal flaw. His information was nearly always presented through the filter of Darwinism. He simply was unable to conceive any other mechanism. Creation, Intelligent Design, and the like were in the domain of fools.

One day after an especially intense period, out of frustration and anger, he shot back at Devadas and said, "Some things you just have to accept as a matter of faith." This response took the boy back to what he had already concluded and opened the door for a discussion about faith – what it was, and what were its strengths and weaknesses.

The subject of origins was ultimately a faith issue, and, in this realm, Kris Gustafson was way over his head. He wished he had never answered so carelessly.

When Devadas first searched the word 'origins,' on his computer, he opened the door to an almost unlimited number of possibilities. He wanted insight into the questions that man has wrestled with for thousands of years, the primeval questions: where we came from, how we are different from animals, etc., etc., etc.

Computers are definitely a Pandora's Box. They enable the user to unlock the world in a manner that has never before existed. The good, the bad, and the ugly can be explored indiscriminately. 'Knowledge at our fingertips!' Were it not for Devadas' focus, he too might have been led astray by the access he had to the world. But in his case, the computer opened alternative sources of information on origins. Some avenues were obviously weird and bizarre which Devad was quick to recognize.

After much study he concluded that the two alternatives he had recognized before were the only ones that made any sense at all. One was the supposition that all happened by naturalistic means, or, to describe it more accurately, "by chance," and the other was that all was planned and executed by some superior intelligence.

Devadas had studied both Latin and Greek and had read many of the stories about the various gods, about how people had made images of metal, wood, stone, and other materials and worshipped them. These gods, as the stories and legends suggested, were able to do amazing things if they wished, but they were also a lot like people with fits of rage, jealousy, love and other emotions.

When he opened the links on God, earth, mankind, and life in general were revealed differently than in the classroom. These views presented this God as the creator and sustainer of all and referenced his existence to what was written in the Bible. Ever since Devadas had been given the Bible by Eliza, he was quite taken by what he read, though frustrated by his lack of understanding. The historical books were interesting, but genealogies left him shaking his head. He instinctively knew that the genealogies were present for

Twice Chosen

a purpose but had not made that connection. He liked the Psalms and was impressed by their intimacy and their authors' obvious love for God.

The latter books of the Old Testament made little sense to him. They addressed the dilemma of a wayward Israel but always predicted a restoration when things would be set straight, but the what, when and how were a mystery.

The New Testament was a different story. Devadas was quite uncertain about the virgin birth and resurrection of Jesus. But the narrative was clear in its presentation, and the subject, Jesus, was the hero - but a very strange hero.

Sometimes after he had finished reading for the day, he would lean back in his chair and think about what he had read, and how it applied to himself and what he was learning in the classroom. The idea of God, or – maybe it was God himself – was increasingly evident in his life.

As he pondered these things, it was evident that Mr. Gustafson rejected all things religious aside from his preoccupation with Darwin. Nothing he had taught or discussed included anything about a personal God who is a Father, or his having a son who came to earth as a baby, or anyone really personal and loving. Furthermore, his mother and the staff never spoke about God – well, Eliza did after he asked her about prayer and then gave him a Bible. He wanted answers, so he decided to talk to his mother while they ate dinner.

Devadas loved dinnertime. It was an opportunity to talk, share, and laugh without interruption by the staff or business. It sometimes was hard to remember that Devadas was so young because of his vocabulary and grasp of so many subjects, but while he could carry on a very adult conversation and could speak and read several languages, he possessed a naivety and innocence that is common to young children. Devadas had a great hunger for his mother's love and acceptance, and she had found a great deal of love to give to this child who had been thrust upon her and who at one time she ignored.

That evening Devadas, when questioned about what he was learning in his classes, told Ellen about his questions regarding the origin of the earth, where people had come from, and his dissatisfaction with the answers received from his teacher. Ellen (for whom all this had little or no meaning) replied gently, "I don't know about such things, but one of these days, as you continue your studies, it will all make sense."

Devadas grew impatient with this response because he wanted his mother to see the inconsistencies and contradictions that he had observed in Mr. Gustafson's explanations and what he had read and understand why it bothered him. But Ellen Smyth couldn't understand his concern, let alone resolve anything. She had received almost no education as a child growing up in England.

Devad then told her about his searching the Internet for input and understanding. Ellen smiled her approval and asked, "And what did you find?"

"Oh, all kinds of things. But there were many that referred to the Bible, Jesus, and how God created us. Why don't we ever talk about these things at The Planes? I looked up the word Bible, and there were a huge number, perhaps millions, of links." He made no mention of the Bible Eliza had given him.

The name of Jesus and the mention of God made Ellen Smyth very uncomfortable, and Devadas could tell because of the dark and uncomfortable look she gave him and the long pause before answering.

When she finally spoke, her voice rose in rebuke. "We don't talk about God or the Bible because it is all a lie. Only the ignorant need God, for he is the last resort of those who can't cope with life. I've repeatedly told my staff to never broach this subject at The Planes. And I'm telling you to forget all this Jesus/God thinking. It is foolishness, and I never want to hear you mention those words again."

But in Ellen Smyth's heart, Devadas' questions had stirred something. She knew God was real. She had taken sides against him many years ago and ever since had tried to push such thoughts from her life to her remorse.

Devadas was hurt. He was hurt by his adopted mother's abruptness and her anger. He was hurt because she had thrust aside his questioning as not being important. But he also noticed something – something. . . . Was it a tear in Ellen Smyth's eye as she looked down at her half eaten plate of food?

The unmistakable conclusion was that someone or something about this place where he had spent all his life was against God and all things about God. Everything else was so good. The staff were his friends, he loved his adopted mother, and he knew she loved him. He had never liked Ms. Borhan. She was strange, and something about her gave him goose bumps. She was always trying to . . . . ., to . . . . ., and he couldn't come up with a word to describe her. And those trips to Madagascar, Jerusalem and taking the Hajj – they were weird.

As he got undressed for bed, he got the urge to pray. He had never been instructed about such things, but he knelt by his bed. It seemed the right thing to do. He prayed, "God or Jesus, what is going on? I'm confused. Help me." And he got up and climbed into bed, his head filled with turmoil. And the words of his prayer were scarcely out of his mouth when he fell asleep.

Chapter 10

PLANS AND INTENTIONS

One morning when Devadas went down to breakfast, he sat by Fred Riley who had come in for a cup of hot coffee. Fred was one of Devadas' best friends, and Devadas often would stop at Fred's little cottage after class where he would play with 'Taffy,' drink hot chocolate, and talk to Fred.

"How are you doing, Buster? You look like you didn't sleep too well last night. Is that Kris Gustafson giving you too much homework?"

Devadas grinned, "Nah!" He said, "I've just been doing a lot of thinking, and last night I couldn't go to sleep for a long time."

"Well, I think you've been studying too hard. I think that you need some exercise and need to get away from the Castle for a while. Aren't you due for your three week break?" Before Devad could answer, Fred continued, "I've been talking with Lady Smyth about a wild idea I have that should fit in with this cr. . ."

He stopped himself from saying crazy, though he didn't think too much of Kris Gustafson, and he couldn't stand Leily Borhan.

". . . ah, curriculum you've been following. The flowers in the high mountains should be magnificent at this time of year, and I was wondering if you and I . . . . ."

And before Fred could finish his sentence, Devad jumped up, knocking over his orange juice in the process, and said loudly, "Yes! Yes! When do we leave?"

"Calm down, youngster. You don't even know where we would be going."

"But going with you would be the greatest," exclaimed Devadas, "and anywhere would be the most fun. Could we climb a mountain?"

One of the girls who helped Eliza in the kitchen scurried into the dining room saying, "What is all the excitement?" Then she saw the spilt orange juice and hurried back to the kitchen to get a cloth to clean it up.

Fred was famous for his ear-to-ear grin, and, with Devadas' excitement, he set a new grin record. "I don't know about climbing a mountain, but we'll be as high or higher than the tallest peaks in the lower 48 states. We'll be hiking but won't have to carry gear, for we'll have porters to do that, and, perhaps, they will use a horse or even a yak to carry everything. I've been fascinated for years in some of the botanists that explored and collected horticultural samples in the Himalayas. We'll be trekking in the same area that Joseph Rock explored during the late 1920's."

Devadas wasn't listening. He was already 10,000 miles away on a high mountain trail in Tibet. "A yak? Isn't that something like a cow?" The idea of carrying their gear on a cow fascinated him. "Will we be sleeping outside – in a tent?"

"Yes, we'll sleep in tents some nights when hiking, but over there it isn't hiking, it is trekking. When we are in villages and cities, we'll stay in hostels, inns, or hotels, maybe even private homes."

Devadas was so excited that he almost forgot he had to get to class. He excused himself and dashed out of the dining room. He had to stop in his own quarters to pick up his books before going upstairs to the classroom area. He could hardly wait to tell Mr. Gustafson. He had totally forgotten all the questions he had when laying in his bed last night.

When he got to the classroom, he couldn't wait to even catch his breath but squealed out, "We're going hiking in the mountains."

"Slow down, young fellow. Who's going hiking, when are you going hiking, and where are you going hiking?"

Devad paused, the last part of the question stopping him. "I don't know where we are going. I never gave him a chance to tell me."

"Who was going to tell you?" said Mr. Gustafson.

"Mr. Riley," answered Devadas.

At this Kris Gustafson laughed and laughed. "Well, it may take you a long time to get there if you don't know where you are going. Actually, Lady Smyth told me of Fred's plan to take you to the Tibet-China area during the three-week break. Fred's interest is in the botany of the area, but Tibet is full of culture and has had a great impact on the world considering its size and isolation. Do you know where Tibet is?"

"In Asia," replied Devadas.

"Right. But where in Asia?" asked his teacher.

Devad answered, "I saw something on TV about the Dalai Lama being in the United States and that he is in exile," not answering the question.

"Right again! And do you know why he is in exile?"

Devadas answered, "Not really. Why?"

"Tibet has been annexed by the People's Republic of China. It is now a Chinese province the Chinese government refers to as 'Tar,' though the cultural Tibet area is much larger. Tar constitutes nearly one-quarter of China in terms of area, but contains only about 0.03% of its population. It is very sparsely populated because of its geography. It has very high mountains and very narrow, deep valleys, not at all conducive to agriculture, travel or industry.

"The Dalai Lama is a title and whoever holds that title is the spiritual and political leader of Tibet. It is because of his influence on the citizens of Tibet that he cannot be allowed to remain in Tibet, for his presence would weaken China's political power in the area."

All this talk about the Dalai Lama and the politics of China and Tibet passed right over Devadas' head. Instead he was picturing hiking – or trekking – through the high mountains with his friend, being followed by all their equipment carried by a cow.

"Wow!"

The possibilities of adventure made him vibrate with excitement.

The rest of the morning passed without Devad hearing much of anything Mr. Gustafson said. Devadas' responses were monosyllables or grunts. When directly called upon, he stumbled along in a manner that said, "I haven't heard a thing."

Kris Gustafson shook his head in frustration and told Devad, "Why don't you run along and see if lunch is ready?"

No time was wasted getting to the dining room. As he slid into his chair, James Simms said, "Hey! I hear you are going to Tibet!"

"News sure gets around fast," said Devad.

"Yeah, I just heard this morning."

"Seems everybody knew about it before I did."

James commented, "Yep, that's what happens in a family. Everybody knows everything about everybody whether it's true of not. What do you think about this?"

Hannah Demaris, always the thoughtful one, said, " It is sure going to be a long flight. I had a friend that flew to Beijing. It took her about 24 hours to get there, counting layovers."

"I don't like to fly," commented Eliza as she entered the room with a platter filled with vegetables. "I like to keep my feet on the ground. I'm content just to oversee the cooking to keep this hungry mob fed." With that she hurried back to the kitchen.

Devadas loved this bantering. These were his friends, and their repartee filled him with the warmth of belonging.

"So, when do you leave?" asked James.

"As soon as the period classes are over, I guess," responded Devad.

"Well, when is that?" James again asked. "I can't keep track of these things."

"It will be a week from Sunday," said Fred, just entering the room. "We have a lot to do to get ready, and we must get this young fellow the proper equipment. The trip will be fun, but it may be wet and cold. I'm not sure what to expect regarding the weather. Anyway, it won't be any picnic. Trekking at elevations between 14,000 and 18,000 feet is going to be hard work." The conversation quieted as all went back to their lunches.

In his room that evening, Devadas toured Tibet via the Internet. Much was advertisement for this or that, but he got a glimpse of the topography and the culture. The land was everything Fred and Mr. Gustafson described, and all seemed on the vertical. Roads were at a minimum, but China has built a railroad that connected Qinghai with Lhasa, and many locations were accessible by air. Agriculture, with the exception of grazing, was nearly nonexistent. The citizens of western China, which included Tibet, were Buddhists, meaning followers of Guatama Buddha, and they believed suffering was universal. Only reaching a higher state of awareness (nirvana) resolved or corrected this condition. However, because of isolation, there were many smaller people groups, most with some combination of Buddhism and Animism.

These details were interesting, but they could not compete with Devadas' excitement about the pending adventure that lay ahead. As he climbed into bed and snuggled under the covers his mind was overflowing with thoughts about fields of beautiful wildflowers surrounded by sharp, snow-covered peaks and deep, shadowy valleys, images soon gone because Devadas with a smile on his face, quickly went to sleep.

೧೨

Sometime during the middle of the night, Devadas' sleep was troubled by a dream in which dark shadows descended on him from all directions. As the shadows drew closer, they appeared to take the shape of people that were not quite human. With the figures came noises, at first distantly with a rattling sound. No. . . it was more a harsh clattering like the sound rats might make scurrying on a metal roof – and the sounds, like the dark figures, closed in until he was encircled by all. His body grew tense with fear and apprehension for something or someone moved so close he could almost feel its breath. It was repugnant, possessive, yet, was familiar, as if seen before.

He felt he was lying on a stage looking up at curtains and drops and then realized he was in a box, not a stage, and he was looking up into a face, a face that filled his mind, his body – his entire being – with evil control. He heard the words, "Nobody wanted you. You will serve me and me only. I have plans for you, and you are mine. . .mine. . . mine. . ."

Then the awareness became louder and louder until he could stand it no longer.

He screamed again and again and again.

The dream, if it was a dream, faded gradually, replaced by the reality of his adopted mother soothing his forehead, and John Hodge, Hannah and Mary next to her. They were all saying at once, "Devadas! What happened? Are you all right?"

Ellen took his hands. "You were thrashing about and screaming. What happened? You're still shaking violently, and your forehead is cold and damp."

Again his mother asked, "What happened?" And she sat down on the bed beside him putting her arms around him, as if in protection.

When Devadas could speak, his voice was slow, low and tremulous. "I don't know! I was asleep when these things and sounds descended on me – and then a face. I was looking up from inside a box. It was a face – a face I'd seen before. I'm sure of it! It stared at me, and its eyes pulled me into his mind saying, 'Nobody wanted you. You are mine. You will serve me, and me only. I have plans for you.' It was awful, and I screamed until I woke up, and you were all here." And his body shook violently, remembering.

Hannah said, "Your screaming woke me. I heard you first and ran for the others. It sounded like someone was torturing you. The cries were awful. I have never heard anything like it." At this Ellen Smyth, Hannah, Mary and John looked at one another with frightened, incredulous expressions.

The next day Ellen Smyth called Hannah, Mary and John to her office. The servants sensed they would be talking to Lady Smyth, for Devadas' dream or vision was truly frightening, and an accurate picture from the past.

"Hannah, Mary, John, what are your reactions to last night?"

Hannah was the first to respond. "Something really strange is going on around here. Whatever else it is, it's something supernatural, it scares me, and I don't like it."

Mary quickly added, "I agree. Frankly, I don't want any part of this. It frightens me and makes my skin crawl. It's not like watching a horror movie. It's something real in here," and she held her hands to her chest. "I'm afraid - afraid for Devadas, and for us all."

Neill Nutter

John Hodge was a widower. He had been with The Planes almost as long as the Smyths had owned the property. One of his sterling characteristics making him an excellent butler was his unflappability. John Hodge was not just unflappable, he was solid, or perhaps 'stolid.'

He spoke. "When I came to The Planes, Lady Smyth instructed me about the house rules. One of those rules was that any mention of God, Jesus, or the church was strictly forbidden. This rule was not an issue for me, for I was not a religious person and, furthermore, was still deeply angered by my wife's untimely death.

My wife Meg, short for Margaret, was a devout Christian, and I loved her dearly. We went to church together, and she was adamant that I needed to become a follower of Christ. I was nearly persuaded. To make the story short, we discovered that she had a lump in her breast that proved to be malignant, a rapidly growing cancer that was incurable.

In less than a year and half, she was gone, despite radiation, drugs, and many all-night prayer vigils. I was furious with God for letting her die. I vowed to never have anything to do with God or the church again."

"I think, based upon all the events that have occurred since Devadas was brought to us, including tonight's dream, that perhaps this house rule should be reevaluated. I know from what we have seen and heard that something evil is occurring, something above and beyond our ability to comprehend. I suspect that it has always been here, but now has become overt and increasingly ominous."

"Furthermore, and, forgive me for my impertinence, I am confident, Lady Smyth, you know more about this than any of us, and that we are entitled to an explanation. Without it I for one will seek other employment."

The range of emotions seen in Ellen Smyth's face ranged from intense anger to great relief. She had been living with this pact made with Satan since she was a teenager, and her fear and pride demanded that she honor it regardless of circumstances. But her love for Devadas had altered everything.

"Won't you all please sit down. I have a story to tell you."

༺༻

"The boy is asking too many questions. We cannot allow him to pursue this avenue. I have plans, but things are not moving as smoothly as I desire. Fortunately, he has been distracted by the pending trip to Tibet. That land is nearly 100% under our control. Meanwhile, if the boy strays too far from the determined path, we must be certain that he encounters an accident. We cannot have him falling into the enemy's camp. He possesses much potential and has the perfect profile to wrest, once and for all, this earth and all its inhabitants from our enemy. Be he also poses a great threat which we can not and will not allow."

∽

After Devadas' dreadful dream, Ellen Smyth and her staff did everything she could to distract the boy from the horror that consumed him. Mary had him play duets with her on the great Steinway in the music room. Simms took him for rides in his 1948 MG TC. But the best distraction was the planned trip to Tibet and western China. There really weren't many days left before their departure. The timing couldn't have been better, and gradually the trip preparations almost crowded out the horrible memories of that night, but not quite.

Chapter 11

TIBET

Their trip to Tibet was, for lack of a better word, long. They flew to Beijing and then to Lhasa. When they landed at Gongar Airport, a representative of the Tibetan travel agency that had planned their itinerary met them. Gongar Airport was very high, about 12,400 feet, and some distance from Lhasa. It wasn't the scenery, outstanding as it was, that took their breath away, it was the elevation. When planning their trip, the travel agency recommended a period for acclimatizing. If their schedule allowed, a week's time adjusting to the elevation at Lhasa wouldn't be too much before trekking, since altitude sickness resulting from low atmospheric pressure – the lack of oxygen and dehydration – was not to be regarded lightly. This was agreeable to Fred because this would enable them to explore the Lhasa area, experience its setting and its culture, and get plenty of rest in a comfortable environment before challenging the strenuous miles and elevation of their proposed trek.

The hotel in which they stayed was once part of a U.S. hotel chain, but now was run by the Chinese government. It was reputed to be the best place to stay in Lhasa with clean rooms and a good selection of food. The beds were especially hard, as were most beds in China. They were pleased that the hotel had western-style toilets. Since much of the trip would be roughing it, they were determined to enjoy their creature comforts.

The setting of Lhasa was not as they had pictured it. Lhasa was a relatively modern city of some 250,000 people, set in a small topographic basin surrounded by mountains and lying on the Kyi chu River. The climate was quite moderate with cool summers and cool but not cold winters. Fred's mental picture was a city perched on a mountain or a plateau, the crowning point being the Potala Palace. He was right about the Palace, but that was all, because Lhasa was located in a basin surrounded by mountains. The palace was located on a hill named Marpo Ri or Red Hill.

Fred and Devadas waited a day before even considering sightseeing. Their first day was spent dealing with jet lag and the elevation. They passed their time dozing, reading about the area, and enjoying the privilege of doing nothing.

The Potala Palace was their first choice of places to visit. They decided to walk rather than take a taxi as the distance from the hotel was only about 1.5 miles. After a couple of blocks, they were regretting their decision. They had to stop often to catch their breath, and once each got a Coca Cola to quench their thirst, maybe not the best, but a familiar choice.

When they got to the Palace, its immensity boggled their minds. It was a huge structure, and they wondered how such a building could have been built without the benefit of machines at such an elevation. As they approached, they saw the steps leading upward to enter the building and looked at each other in disbelief.

"What do you think, partner? Do you want to try?"

Devadas answered, "We must. Our visitor pass is for this morning. If we don't go now, we may have to wait two or three days."

Fred clenched his jaw in anticipation and responded, "Right you are. They only allow about 1500 visitors per day. Let's get going, but not too fast."

With many stops to let their lungs and hearts come to equilibrium, they were able to pass through the portico and into the courtyard where the Dalai Lamas watched Tibetan opera. From there they entered into the White Palace where the administrative offices had been and where the Dalai Lama had lived.

The Red Palace was the worship center and had many chapels. The Palace was a great museum. Of the many floors, 1,000 rooms, and myriad murals, statues, shrines, and stupas, (mounds or structures where the tombs of the esteemed were located), they were quickly exhausted – physically, and mentally as well. There was so much to see, and the views out the windows were spectacular. Somewhere they had read that a person needed at least two and a half hours to see the Palace. In their opinion a visitor needed two and a half days.

Before attempting to go back to their hotel, they stopped in the central pavilion to purchase a book describing the Palace, so they might remember what they had seen. Fortunately, they were able to buy copies in English.

Twice Chosen

They wisely decided to catch a taxi back to the hotel, and, though the ride took only a few short minutes, Fred kept dozing off. Devadas' excitement kept him awake, and soon they were back at the hotel. They decided to go to the café that specialized in hamburgers for lunch. Trying to eat was a mistake for neither of them was able to eat a thing. It wasn't that the burgers didn't taste like McDonalds. They were simply too tired to eat.

After lunch they took a nap. Fred didn't go to sleep right away, but Devad did. Fred noted that the boy tossed and turned an unusual amount. After perhaps an hour Devadas roused and commented that his stomach hurt. Fred encouraged him to try to relax, thinking that the excitement, the exertion and the elevation were working together making him feel ill. Devad closed his eyes and tried to lay still. This lasted for perhaps ten minutes until he jumped up, crying out: "I've got to go to the bathroom." He barely made it before he had the dry heaves.

After his stomach settled a bit, he went back and lay on his bed, commenting, "I don't feel very good."

Fred came over and felt his head: "You don't seem to have a fever," he said "Do you hurt anywhere?"

Devadas shook his head. "No! But, oh, shaking my head made me dizzy. Everything is going round and round."

By this time Fred was getting concerned. He thought, "This boy has altitude sickness. I'm going to call room service and see if there is a doctor." He walked over to the phone and dialed the desk. "Do you have a doctor on call?"

The answer was in Chinese and he understood nothing.

"English, please! English, please!"

There was a pause, and another person's voice came on the line in broken English: "May I help you?"

"Yes, we need a doctor. Do you have a doctor in the hotel?"

While Fred was still on the phone, Devadas again rushed to the bathroom and emptied the limited contents of his stomach. Fred put down the phone. "They do have a doctor, and he will be here in a few minutes. I want you checked. The elevations we will be hiking are at least as high as here, and I can't run the risk of having you suffering from altitude sickness where there is no help or convenient means of getting you to a lower elevation."

He'd just finished telling Devadas his concern when there was a tap on the door. When Fred opened the door, he was met by a diminutive Chinese man wearing wire rim glasses and carrying a leather valise.

In good English he asked: "You have a young man that is ill?"

"Yes, he is over here on the bed. He just vomited. He doesn't seem to have a fever, but he is definitely sick. We are planning to go trekking in a couple of days, and, if this is altitude sickness, I question whether this would be a good idea."

"You are absolutely right. The high passes are not for those suffering from altitude illness. Let me examine him."

He set his valise by the bed and took out several items, including his stethoscope.

"Unfasten your belt so I can feel your stomach. Hm! Seems rather bloated. Now pull up your shirt. I want to listen to your lungs. Unhuh! Good! I want to check your temperature. Open your mouth. This is an old style glass thermometer. Don't bite on it, and keep your mouth shut. We don't have any of those thermometers that are placed in your ear as they do in the States."

After a couple of minutes, he removed the thermometer and read it. "Hm! Good! It is only slightly elevated, 37.2 degrees Celsius, just about 99 degrees Fahrenheit. Now let me look in your ears. Hm. Have you been dizzy?"

Devadas nodded his head and then groaned.

"When did you arrive? Did you come via Beijing?"

The doctor straightened and turned toward Fred. "I don't believe he has anything serious, and I'm quite sure it is not altitude illness. His lungs sound normal, and his breathing is not labored. I believe that he had some problems with barometric pressure on the flight, causing dizziness. That in turn would exacerbate any tendencies for nausea. His stomach is quite firm. It is my opinion his stomach is upset from something he has eaten. That, coupled with jet lag and a small bit of fluid in his inner ear from the flight or a slight infection, has combined to create his discomfort. I think he will be doing much better by tomorrow. If he isn't, have the desk contact me."

With that he gathered his things to leave, giving Fred his card.

"How is it that you speak such good English," asked Fred.

"I did two internships at Johns Hopkins University."

"Well, that explains it. Thank you, doctor, for your assistance and opinions." He let the good doctor out the door.

"Well, Champ, how are you feeling? I'm encouraged that we will be able to hike, rather trek, as planned."

"Me too," added Devadas, "and I do feel better since I got rid of the stuff in my stomach."

‍ ‍

They spent the day before leaving for their trek taking a tour of the city. They had already seen the Palace, but, to conserve their energy, a guided tour seemed the right thing to do. They were able to schedule a private tour with a person recommended by the clerk at the desk.

When the guide arrived in the morning, he was driving an ancient Peugeot. He first took them to the Drepung monastery nearly five miles from the hotel. At one time Drepung had more than 7,000 monks and was the largest monastery in the world. Today, with the Chinese government controlling the number, it had only a few hundred. The monastery continued in exile in South India.

In the afternoon they went to the Jokhang Temple. The temple was the most sacred temple in Tibet and held the Jowo Shakyamuni Buddha statue, the most venerated object in Tibetan Buddhism.

Devadas could not help but compare the Jokhang Temple with the Masjid Al Haram mosque in Mecca. Jokhang Temple was very colorful and artistic with the Buddhas and other icons. It was large with typical prayer wheels, frescoes, and beautiful colored silk hangings. The appearance of the temple was in the ancient Buddhist style of Nepal and India with sloped roofs, with all parts concave to the sky and, frequently, with religious statues on them.

The Masjid Al Haram mosque had been equally beautiful but in a different way. It was majestic and much larger than the Temple with a great open courtyard, and it could accommodate millions of worshippers at one time. Its artistic design was accomplished with shapes – for example arches, columns, and the seven minarets. Tile and polished rock were used extensively, especially marble. Images of people were totally absent, for Islam forbids any kind of representation of what Allah has created.

Devadas noted one similarity however. Their guide had explained to them that Buddhists often made pilgrimages to Jokhang Temple. As part of their pilgrimage, they were expected to make three trips in and around the temple – the first inside the temple and two on prescribed routes around it. The outer loop now twice crossed over a busy new highway, the Beijing Lam, so was not taken as often as in the past. In addition to the circuits around the temple, obeisance also includes frequent prostration, recitation of mantras and the spinning of prayer wheels.

Devadas wondered how walking around a shrine or temple benefited the walker, other than the exercise. "I suppose they are trying to impress God," he said to Fred, who answered, I don't get it either. I guess it is whatever works for them."

"But," continued Devadas, "why would they spend the money to come here and go to such great effort?"

Fred scratched his head. "I've never thought much about these things – not for a long time anyway. When I was a kid, I went to Sunday school and church with my folks."

"Why don't you do that now?" asked Devad.

"After I went to college, I was really turned off by religion." Devadas started to ask another question, but their guide, seeing their interest in pilgrimages, began to explain.

"Buddhism is a very old religion, much older than Christianity. Buddha is the 'enlightened one,' for that is what the name means. He realized that suffering is universal and caused by desire or lust. The cure to suffering is to eliminate desire in eight steps by having the "right": the right viewpoint, the right aspiration the right speech, the right behavior, the right occupation, the right effort, the right mindfulness and right meditation. The idea is to achieve harmony – harmony with yourself, with others, with your surroundings, with everything. Everything is one. When we die, our soul is reborn, and we are able to continue working toward harmony. Eventually we reach nirvana."

"Then these walks, prostrations and prayers are all part of accomplishing the eight steps?" asked Fred.

"Yes!" answered their guide.

"When will they reach nirvana?" asked Devadas.

To this their guide merely shook his head, indicating that he didn't know.

"And if you reach nirvana, what then?" asked Fred,

The guide broke into a wide Tibetan grin, "Maybe you become a Buddha."

Just to the north of the Jokhang Temple was the great square where the market was located. This was to be their last stop for the day, and they were already tired, again caused by the elevation. On the square were many vendors' stands where one could purchase rugs, clothes, gold and silver, almost anything Tibetan.

Their guide said, "You must buy some Thangkas. See? Like this."

He walked to a stand and picked up a scroll-like fabric painting. "They are very beautiful."

The one he held up for them was perhaps 18 inches wide and somewhat longer. It was a heavy, dark red – almost maroon-colored – a velvet material, with a man embroidered on it as a picture. It was gold in color as if made of gold leaf.

"Very nice," said their guide, "A Bodhisattva."

"What is a Bodhisattva?" asked Fred and Devad as one.

"A Bodhisattva is one who is almost a Buddha, a very enlightened one. Come with me. I have a friend who will give you the best value."

"I'm not interested," said Devadas, exhausted.

"Nor I," added Fred.

"How about a Tibetan sword?" asked their guide, eager to get them to buy anything.

"No." said Fred. "I think we have seen enough, and, besides, we are really bushed – er, tired. We would like you to return us to our hotel."

Their guide was obviously disappointed, for he had hoped to profit from his taking them to the market. "How about Tibetan medicine, or herbs like snow lotus, or saffron?" asked the guide hopefully.

Again, Fred and Devadas said no and asked again to return to their hotel. This time their guide complied.

At the hotel, Fred gave their guide a generous tip, and he drove away quite pleased after all after his day guiding these two Americans.

Their day had been full, and they were glad to sit and relax. That evening they ate in the Chinese restaurant in the hotel. The food was excellent, and they were finally hungry. It appeared that they were adjusting to their environment.

Before going to bed, Devadas found a hotel computer, and he emailed his adopted mother back at The Planes.

Chapter 12

S<small>URPRISE</small>!

Both Devad and Fred woke early. After a hurried breakfast of rolls and tea, they organized and reorganized their gear in preparation for the trip to the airport and their flight to Xichang in Sichuan Province. Their flight would take about two hours, and then they would meet their host/guide who would accompany them on their trek.

Their guide Lee, his Chinese name, greeted the travelers as they disembarked from the plane in Xichang. He was a sturdy, well built man of medium height with dark twinkling eyes. His English was quite good, and his dress was western. After introductions the three of them gathered their luggage off the tarmac, where it had been unloaded, and carried it to his old Jeep.

Xichang was a modern city with a population of over 100,000 people. It was linked to the rest of China not only by air, but by highway and rail. It was a city that had entered the space age; northwest of the city was one of China's satellite launching sites.

Lee explained that from Xichang they would drive by Jeep to Qiaowa. Qiaowa was about 60 miles west of Xichang, but the road to get there took a big swing to the south before heading north and had many twists and turns, going about 150 miles in the process. In Qiaowa they would stay in an inn. From there they would ride horseback to the first tent camp. After that they would be on foot or take public transportation until they reached Zhongdian (now called Shangri-la) in Yunnan Province, which was the end of their journey. Given the trail conditions and the repeated changes in elevation of 4000 feet or more, to go farther than ten kilometers per day was all they should expect.

The journey to Qiaowa was breathtaking but long. The first few vistas and hairpin turns held their attention, but it wasn't long before the magnitude of the scenery around them dulled the senses. It was a good thing that neither Fred nor Devadas suffered from motion sickness, or the journey would have been misery, seeming without end. Talk was difficult. The Jeep was noisy and had no top. Fred sat in the front with Lee, and Devadas was squeezed in the back with their luggage. Since the tailgate had been let down to extend the storage space, he could at least see over the load.

The trip Fred had planned, besides being an adventure, was ostensibly to take pictures of the flora and to take notes about their ecosystems. Southeastern China has one of the most varied flora of any place in the world, and botanists, such as Joseph Rock, had introduced hundreds and perhaps thousands of species to the United States from that region.

While Fred was busy with his photography, Devadas would be on his own, busily sketching whatever captured his interest, or otherwise investigating their surroundings. He, too, found plants fascinating and loved recording the details of their structure, something that Fred sometimes asked him to do. Mostly, Devadas, fascinated by everything he saw, drew for the love of drawing, so his drawings would be a pictorial journal of their trip.

The night at the Inn in Qiaowa was not especially comfortable. Besides a hard bed, the food was at best, 'interesting.' Whatever it was, it contained lots of chili peppers, potatoes, and some kind of mystery meat. Fred was able to use some high potency beverage to help wash down his dinner, but Devadas was not given that privilege. A Coke had to suffice. Lee seemed to relish whatever it was they were eating, and he too drank from one of those ubiquitous red and white cans of American beverage.

Early in the morning they met Lee in the dining room. He no longer wore western clothes, but was dressed in the clothing of the locals. After they again loaded their belongings in the Jeep, they drove some miles to the outskirts of Qiaowa to what passed as a barn or stable. When they drove up, a young man emerged from the barn and cheerfully greeted them all in an unfamiliar tongue. When asked, Lee said the language was Lisu. He then introduced them to his assistant whose Chinese name was Huan. Huan did not speak English, so they shook hands and smiled their greetings.

Lee instructed them to unload, and, as soon as they did, he parked the Jeep in one of the bays of the building. After that he and his helper brought three small, sturdy, shaggy horses to a rail where they were tied. Blankets were then put over the horses, and wooden pack frames were placed on their backs for securing gear.

Twice Chosen

Devadas disappointedly asked Lee, "I was in hopes you would use Yaks for carrying the gear."

Lee laughed as he worked. "Yaks are sturdy and reliable, but horses are faster, and can be comfortably ridden if necessary and besides they are more intelligent. I find them a much better choice."

While Fred and Devadas' belongings were packed in red nylon packs suitable for both carrying on their backs or by hand, Lee's gear was packed in sturdy leather bags.

Lee and his assistant were very careful about putting the loads on the packhorses. When satisfied that all was in order, they again went inside and returned with four horses that would be their mounts. Fred asked, "Why are you saddling four horses? Is your assistant going with us?"

Lee replied, "When we get to our first camp, Huan will lead our mounts back here. We will continue on foot, leading the packhorses."

The saddles they used were something like western saddles, but not quite the same. The pommels were quite high, but none had a horn like a U.S. western saddle. They were as lightweight as an English saddle, but also were well constructed and built for comfort. After the bridles were fitted, the group was nearly ready to leave.

Since Devadas had never ridden horseback, he was given the gentlest horse and shown how to put his foot in the stirrup. With a bit of a boost, he was able to get in the saddle. His instructions were, "Just hang on. Don't worry about guiding or controlling the horse, and don't jerk on the reins."

Fred had ridden on a couple of occasions but felt nearly as apprehensive as Devadas. He, too, received essentially the same instructions.

It had been light for several hours when they finally hit the trail. Lee led the way, leading the three pack animals. Behind them followed Devadas, then Fred, and bringing up the rear was Huan.

The ride to their first camp would take about six hours. There they would be staying in a tent, and Devad was looking forward to that experience. Riding a horse was fine, but sleeping outside – almost outside anyway – was something he had been looking forward to since Fred had first mentioned the trip. Devad had slept in the huge tent when on the Hajj, but that was different. There he had been with Ms. Borhan and surrounded by hundreds, maybe thousands, of pilgrims. Here in the mountains they would be completely by themselves, and that isolation was exciting, if even a bit frightening.

Lee was an experienced, licensed trekking guide and had been recommended to them. He had been leading small trekking groups for nearly ten years, so they had confidence in him and his judgment. They were sure that the accommodations awaiting them would protect them from the weather, and, with their sleeping bags and pads, they would be comfortable and not get too cold.

The trail first led across meadows, Lee called them 'cattle fields,' until they began to climb up the range that hemmed in that side of the valley. The trail was steep and rocky. Devadas called to Lee and asked, "Is this trail like the ones we will be walking on?"

Lee called back, "Some better, some worse."

At this response Devadas made a face.

After a while, the travelers weren't sure which they would rather do, walk or ride. Their bottoms and legs were aching and sore. They just didn't fit the shape of the saddle or the horse's back. Still, both Fred and Devad knew if they had been walking, they would have been going very slow, having to stop every dozen yards or less to catch their breath.

The horses steadily plodded along, seemingly unfazed by the narrowness, steepness, or rockiness of the trail. They weren't even breathing hard. Most of the time Fred and Devad were able to enjoy the view, but their enjoyment was limited by places where they feared to look down because the trail was so narrow and the slope so steep, rocky, and long, that it seemed all might tumble into the valley. And then there were the numerous aches and pains from their bodies trying to adjust to the shape of the saddles. Fred took numerous pictures, so he and Devadas could one day see the scenery in a more comfortable setting.

Lunch stop was in a broad, open basin. Fred and Devadas were ready for a break. After Devadas dismounted, he could barely walk. He walked like he was crippled. Fred watched him and laughed, but, after he dismounted, it was Devad's turn to laugh.

They were above tree line, and their surroundings were rocky, sparsely covered with low, ground-hugging clumps of flowers and a few low shrubby trees, and it was gloriously beautiful. Running water from recently melted snow ran down the slopes in rivulets and onto the trail. The sounds of the running water and the greetings of small birds filled the air with music. It was beautiful: the vistas, the earth spreading in all directions and, in the far distance, cloud crowned peaks. To top it all off were the scents of the high mountain tundra, the moist ground, and the air descending from snowfields and glaciers.

Huan removed the gear from the horses, one at a time, then brushed and hobbled them so they could not wander away while they browsed and drank greedily from the numerous rills of running water. While Huan was busy with the horses, Lee proceeded to prepare lunch. He lit a small kerosene stove and heated water for tea. He had western-style, freeze-dried soup for the travelers, but for Huan and himself he made a gruel from something that looked like dry hot cereal and added it to his cup of hot tea. Then he produced a dollop of yak butter and some sugar which he added, stirred, and drank like a thick soup.

Devadas wanted to know what they were eating, and Lee said, "We call it tsampa. It is made from toasted ground barley. Would you like to try some?"

Devadas smelled Lee's cup with the sour cream yak butter. The smell made him turn up his nose, and he shook his head.

"No thanks."

Instead, Fred and Devad enjoyed what Lee had brought for them. Lee also gave them some big crackers he called pilot bread that helped soak up the soup and fill their stomachs. They too had tea, but with sugar, not yak butter.

After they had eaten, they were chilled and got their fleece jackets from their gear. Huan rounded up the horses, and then he and Lee repacked the gear and saddled their mounts. Devadas could barely climb into his saddle. It was much harder then when they had begun their trip.

In late afternoon they descended to an open area that contained a tent. It had obviously been erected for some time, for the grass and vegetation around it were well beaten down. It wasn't canvas but appeared to be a fabric woven of fur or hair. Lee said it was yak hair. It looked something like an umbrella tent but supported by many external poles and ropes. It didn't look like any tent Fred had seen.

"What about rain?" asked Fred.

"The top is in two layers," explained Lee. "The upper or outer portion blocks off most rain, and the lower or inner roof blocks what might leak through the top. It has to rain very hard for any to get inside."

Huan unloaded the gear from the packhorses and put it in the tent. He then brushed and hobbled the horses and let them free to drink and browse. He turned next to the riding horses, loosened the saddles, and tied them into a pack string to return to town. Leading the way on his horse with the others following, he headed back up the trail for Qiaowa. It would be dark before he had the horses back in the barn, and his would be a late supper. He waved his goodbyes as he rode away.

"I'm going to like this," said Devadas to no one in particular. Because the door flap was open, he wobbled into the tent, checking everything carefully. He found a container with food, potatoes, chili peppers, a couple of containers of what looked a bit like sauerkraut a box of freeze-dried trail food, and other items.

On the table was a small, well-worn book. Since the printing was in Chinese, Devad wasn't sure what it was, but it reminded him of the Bible that had been given him by Eliza. He knew he must remember to ask Lee about it.

The space in the tent was divided in two areas. A small, round metal stove was set up at the end where the door was, and to one side was a small folding table and several three- legged folding stools. At the other end there were hides and rough blankets on the ground. This was, presumably, where they were to place their sleeping bags. It was quite cozy and had a noticeable outdoorsy smell. When inside, you didn't get the direct brunt of the wind, although it did blow under the edges, for the tent had no floor. For lighting there was a single kerosene lamp over the table that swung back and forth as the tent yielded to every breath of wind.

While Devad was checking the tent and their overnight accommodations, Fred was trying to help Lee with chores. He had gone to get water from a spring nearby. He could see that Lee was in shape, for the ride had no effect on him at all, or not so he noticed, while carrying the bucket of water was about all that Fred could manage.

"I am so stiff," said Fred. "I hope we can get comfortable so we can sleep tonight."

"You will do just fine," responded Lee. "I will fix you both a cup of herbal tea that contains white willow bark. It is the predecessor of aspirin and completely safe, and, besides, it tastes good."

Lee fixed supper over the unusual stove. It was actually a can within a can and used charcoal briquettes for fuel. It was very efficient, and, once lighted, cooked their dinner quickly.

Devadas and Fred were very hungry, and the food tasted very good. The meal contained potatoes and onions with a sauce containing beef which tasted spicy and gingery. It was set off by something sour and spicy, like Korean kimchi. They also had tea, though both Devad and Fred declined the dollop of yak butter that Lee offered and found so tasty.

As the sun went down, it became quite cool, and, outside, the wind picked up. They could feel the currents of air, so they once again put on jackets. The stove was the only source of heat, and they sat close so they could visit until time to retire.

Fred asked Lee where he had learned to speak such good English.

"I was attending university in Chengdu, working on a degree in engineering. On a bulletin board I saw a notice about an American who was teaching an 'ESL English' class – English as a second language. I decided to sign up. Later, I took formal classes in English.

"ESL was not my first exposure to English as I had grown up in the mountains of Yunnan Province where, years ago, missionaries had come from North America. My grandfather was one of their first converts. As a result of his enthusiasm, he became a language helper. In the process of helping the missionaries learn their language, he also learned some English.

"When he became a convert, he quit drinking. Many of our countrymen spent much of their time drunk, both men and women, but after their conversions, their lives changed dramatically, and they prospered. My own father became a storeowner, and it was because of his enthusiasm for education that I went to the university in Chengdu.

"Back to my story – I went to the ESL class taught by a young woman. It was very informal yet informative. She would ask us questions about ourselves, and we would ask her questions. She had us read English newspapers and books. We even sang American songs. During the class we found out she was a Christian, so we had the opportunity to ask her many questions about her faith. We would sometimes meet in a tearoom or for dinner, as well as in the regular class. We all became friends. She was in Chengdu for a year. Many of us still correspond with her back in the States.

"Anyway, as a result of her witness and that of my father and my grandfather, I began to consider Christianity. I had no faith. Many of my people, the Lisu, are Christians, but there remain those who believe in what you might call witchcraft. For example, when someone becomes ill, they will go to the Shaman rather than to a doctor. Others still worship spirits rather than the one true God.

"As I said, I began to examine Christianity and began reading the Bible. What I read made a lot of sense to me. I was controlled by lusts and desires. I had always focused on self, and what the Bible said about man being a sinner described me exactly. Then I remembered my grandfather's stories about how it was with the Lisu people before the missionaries, John and Isobel Kuhn, came to tell them about Jesus. I think that being an engineer has advantages because I looked at all the evidence, and there was only one logical conclusion. I needed Jesus Christ, and one night I knelt by my bedside, confessed that I was a sinner, and committed myself to Him."

Devadas' eyes glistened.

"Then what I saw on the table when I came in was a Bible."

"Yes," was Lee's rejoinder. "That is my Bible. Actually it was my grandfather's, but, after he died, it was given to me."

"I thought China didn't allow Christianity," interrupted Fred.

Lee answered carefully, "China is very careful about all religions, even Buddhism and the other ancient religions. The authorities regard Christianity as a western religion, and, therefore, it is especially suspect. Furthermore, Buddhism and the other religions do not, as you say, 'upset the apple cart.' Tibet is an exception, but the issue there is not Buddhism. It is the country's rebellion against China's claim to Tibet, the claim that China should govern

Tibet and not the Dalai Lama who insists on independence, thus forcing him to live in exile in India."

"Christianity claims that we are all children of God, and, therefore, our allegiance is first and foremost to Him and his Son Jesus Christ. Look at it from the standpoint of a country always watchful for dissenters. The rulers see Christianity as a threat because the Christian's allegiance is to Christ and not the State. Another concern is that Christians endorse a standard of behavior that becomes a threat to corruption in government, regardless of country or geography. The third factor is that we are in a spiritual battle and are even hated. This is what is spoken about in the Bible, in Chapter Six of the book of Ephesians. There it says, 'Our struggle is not against flesh and blood, but against the rulers, authorities, and powers of this dark world, and against the spiritual forces of evil in the heavenly realms.'"

"Do you really believe all this stuff?" asked Fred, voicing incredulity.

"Yes I do. And I didn't come to my convictions easily or lightly. My decision to surrender myself to the Sovereign God came after much thought and soul searching. As I said before, I saw my life going nowhere. I saw the results of the new life in my family and my people. And, that young woman who came to China to teach English as a second language loved us. Furthermore, the Bible speaks truthfully. It is as simple as that."

Devadas spoke up. "Fred, when we were in the Jokhang Temple in Lhasa, and we were talking about pilgrimages and things people do to win the favor of God, you said something like, 'When I was a kid, I went to Sunday school and church with my folks, but after I went to college, I was really turned off by religion.' What did you mean by that?"

Fred thought for a moment.

"Remember that I was a biology . . . , well, I was actually a botany student, and we were shown how evolution explained where life came from, and how it developed through time. Who needs God to explain things? Also, I was just a kid, and my professors were Ph.D.s. They knew what they were talking about, and I was just out of high school. I was impressed with their knowledge. They showed us that Christianity was just a myth. Adam and Eve, the flood, and even Jesus were just stories that educated people dismissed as sentimental tripe."

Lee piped up, "Evolution was also drummed into my head during my entire education, and that was one of the reasons I had no faith, even if my parents and grandparents did. They were just ignorant mountain people. But that's another advantage of being an engineer. In engineering you discover that nothing happens by chance or by accident. Any complicated machine requires a designer, whether living or mechanical. Things don't happen by accident."

Twice Chosen

Devadas turned again to Fred, "Didn't you question what you were being taught? I do! When Dr. Gustafson tells me something in class, or I read something in one of my books that has a lot of words like 'could be,' 'might be,' or 'may be possible,' and so on, I start asking questions."

Fred shrugged and said, "I was naïve, and to me evolution, for instance, makes more sense then someone you can't see creating the whole universe. You know, Devad, I envy you a bit. You have been given so much intelligence and a lot of common sense besides."

"Well, you should take another look at your basic suppositions," scolded Devad.

Devadas then shuddered. "I can't prove it, but what Lee said about the powers of this dark world and the spiritual forces of evil in the heavenly realms must have something to it. Remember that terrible dream I had not long before we left on our trip? It was definitely something evil. I don't understand it, but I will tell you this. I hate it.

The words were barely out out of Devadas' mouth when the ground began shaking violently.

"Earthquake," shouted Lee, "a bad one."

The stove tipped over, striking Devad on the leg, and the lantern fell from its hook at the roof of the tent. It almost hit him on the head, but landed and broke on the ground beside him, the kerosene spilling and catching fire. All three rushed out the door flap. Neither Devad nor Fred had ever experienced anything like this. They were dizzy and nauseous from the earth's shaking.

Outside, starlight filled the heavens, and there was a crescent of moon, but the rumble of falling rock could be heard in the distance, sounding like thunder. The packhorses were struggling against their hobbles and crying out their fright in anguished whinnies. In five minutes or less, the earthquake was over. The sky had not changed. It was as if nothing had happened. Even the horses had quieted, but were still obviously restless.

Now, the fire in the tent became their concern. Fueled by the kerosene, the fire had set the stools and table ablaze and was climbing up the center tent pole. In addition, a container with provisions was also burning. Since the tent had no floor, it was spreading across the beat down vegetation toward the sleeping area.

Lee slashed an opening at the end of the tent with his knife and began pulling their belongings to safety. Included with the gear was a bucket, so Fred grabbed it and hurried to the spring for water. One bucket suppressed the flames, and a second bucket was enough to extinguish it entirely, though a third was thrown on the area for good measure.

With the lantern gone and the fire out, they had nothing but the light from the night sky, so they scrambled through their gear for flashlights.

"Is everybody all right?" queried Lee when the excitement had waned.

"The lamp almost hit me and the stove did, but I wasn't burned," spoke up Devadas.

"I never want to go through anything like that again," exclaimed Fred.

"You will," commented Lee, "Any big quake will have aftershocks for days, some almost as severe as the original, so we'll have to get used to it. But, we never will. They are always a surprise and frightening. For the remainder of our trip, I think we will sleep in the open. We definitely won't sleep in any buildings, even if there are any left standing."

With their flashlights they were able to organize their gear. They opened door of the tent, got rid of the smoke, and helped air out some of the smell. Where the fire had been was a sodden mess. The hides and blankets that were on the ground to the side were not burned, and, other then the rancid odor of smoke and kerosene, everything was all right. They could sleep in the tent if the smell wouldn't be an issue, so they set about picking up the broken glass by flashlight, straightening the stove, carrying out the burnt debris, and letting it continue to air. Finally, they were able to open their bags and lay them out. After getting snuggled in for the night, they lay awake for a long time, being reminded by the smell and their memory of the earth violently shaking.

It had been a most eventful evening.

The sun rose right on time, but it took a while for the trekkers to awaken. Lee knew what lay ahead and was first to arise. It took a while to get Devadas and Fred to wake up. Once out of their bags, they had to find their clothes and get into their hiking boots. As they stood up and surveyed the results of the earthquake by daylight, all seemed relatively in order. The tent was what bore the brunt of the previous nights excitement. The inside still smelled pretty bad. The main tent pole was charred, but otherwise was serviceable, and the end where Lee had slashed a new opening, could be patched and sewed.

Lee sighed as he examined the situation. "It can all be repaired or replaced. I have used this same tent and this same spot for three years. I set it up after the snow is gone, and in the late summer after the last trekkers are gone I come and get it." He sighed and shook his head and muttered something that sounded like, "All things work together for good . . . " and his voice dropped so the others couldn't hear him.

"I hope and pray that Huan is all right, and the Jeep and horses are not buried beneath the barn, but sadly I have no way to find out. Out here cell phones don't work. There are no cell towers, and I haven't been able to afford a satellite cell phone."

The original plan was to continue on foot to the next camping spot, leading the pack string. The elevations were too high for the American tenderfeet to carry all their gear as well as their photography equipment and art supplies.

"I'm worried about what lies ahead," said Lee as he was packing the horses.

"Why?" asked Devadas.

"The trail is steep, and there are many places where slides could totally remove the trail. If so, we won't be able proceed but will have to return to our camp here and then plan some other strategy."

It had been daylight for a couple of hours when they finally hit the trail. Lee said that he usually followed with the horses, having the trekkers go first, but this time because of the potential for the trail being unstable, he wanted to be in the front. This meant that the trekkers would have to watch where they walked, but it was better than being on a hillside that might go sliding down several thousand feet into the valley.

The day was beautiful when they began with a vivid, penetrating blue sky, but, as the day progressed, more and more clouds appeared – a typical summer day in the mountains. When Fred and Devadas stopped to catch their breath or do photography, the horses would grow impatient as if they knew something the others didn't. They stopped quite often, for they were at least 12,000 feet elevation or higher, and this trail was not smooth and barrier free like the streets of Lhasa. It was rocky and narrow with lots of melt water to negotiate. There were few trees, and what were there stood windblown and scrubby. Fred thought they looked like the sub-Alpine Firs and White Bark Pines in the western U.S. The rocky surface, where more dry and sunny, held a profusion of tiny, ground-hugging wildflowers like those seen the day before. Fred was in seventh heaven, but, since Devadas' sketching took more time than Fred's pictures, he didn't get much time to draw.

They had been out about three hours when they came to a place where the trail had literally been carved into a cliff. Because of the precipitous rock slope, it was the only way the trail could continue. They had no idea of who would go to such trouble for it was a major engineering feat. The trail was narrow, only a few feet wide, if that, and it dropped abruptly for a long way, at least several hundred feet and maybe more. The bottom could not be seen without looking over the edge, and neither Fred nor Devadas were brave enough to try.

Lee and the horses stopped abruptly, and he called back, "Trouble! The trail is gone."

"What do we do now?" asked the hikers in unison.

"We have to go back, and I don't know if I can. The trail is too narrow for me to go around the horses, or for the horses to turn around. Not only is the trail narrow, but there are fractures in the rock where I stand. This part of the trail could go at any instant. I want the two of you to retrace your steps back to where the trail is wide enough to turn the horses around. I know these animals, and they are mountain horses, but I've never been in this situation. I need your prayers. NOW!"

Then, Lee began talking quietly to his horses.

The lead horse, the one directly behind Lee, was not happy with the situation, the rock, the trail or lack thereof, and wanted to turn around, which with all the gear was quite impossible. Lee was urging the rear horse to back down the trail, and the horse, well knowing what was expected of it, was not cooperating. It couldn't see behind itself, even by turning its head, and it was too cautious to back up without knowing where the trail was located.

Lee had the presence of mind to keep a light grip on the lead rope of the horse directly behind him. The other two horses were tied, one behind the other, so all three horses were, in effect, linked together. Lee was praying fervently because his life and the life of the horses were all at stake, and even if one horse fell from the trail, it would likely take the other two with it and all their gear and food would be lost.

Lee knew where his eternal destiny lay if he were killed, but what about these two with him? Without food, not knowing the local languages, and with so much of the country devastated by the massive quake, he didn't think they would have a very good chance at survival. Furthermore, there were known to be ruffians that would be take advantage of the quake to loot and kill, and Fred's cameras would be very desirable.

His prayers were intense and in Lisu, the language of his youth.

Fred and Devad were waiting well back on the trail, not understanding the seriousness of Lee's situation. They had wanted adventure, but this was a bit more than they had bargained for.

Fred and Devadas knew by the tone of his voice that Lee was in trouble, and they also realized that if something happened to their guide, they were in trouble. Fred cried out, "How do I pray? What do I say?"

Devadas answered, and this was the advantage of being young, "Just tell God that we're in trouble, and we need his help."

It is said that when a man is drowning, his whole life flashes before his eyes. Lee wasn't drowning, but he felt death breathing down his neck. He regretted many of his decisions: that he hadn't sent Fred and Devadas on ahead or left the horses with them; that he hadn't checked out the trail by himself, allowing them to turn the horses around in a less precarious location. He was sorry that he had horses. Mules were much more sensible animals.

He was sorry that they hadn't returned to Qiaowa. He was sorry they hadn't stayed in the tent camp and tried to make the best of it until help came. Regrets came fast and furious, but they only made matters worse. Things were as they were. He couldn't go back in time. God's will would be done. And, with this acknowledgment, God's peace swept over him, and he relaxed and prayed aloud, "Lord God, I give you this situation. You are in charge."

At that moment came the aftershock he had told the others would happen. At the other end of the slide, more trail disappeared in the thunderous roar and dust of falling rock. The lead horse reared and wheeled in panic, and in so doing caused the rope that tied the three together to jerk the second horse, which lunged backward into the last horse. The result was that all three horses lost their footing, plunged off the trail, and fell down into the abyss with all the food and gear. Lee leaned back into the rock wall and sank down on his haunches. He had never been so frightened. The only words he could utter were "Oh God, oh God, oh God!"

All of this action was out of Fred and Devadas' line of sight. When the aftershock came, they both cried out in fear. The sound of rocks falling drowned out the horses' screams as they tumbled over the edge and through the air. All they heard was a distant crash somewhere far below them and silence.

They had no idea what happened to Lee. Had he fallen, swept off the trail with the rocks? What about the horses? They carefully hurried forward with fear and anticipation. As they rounded the bend, they saw Lee in a fetal position, completely still.

"Lee, Lee, are you all right?"

At the sound of their voices, he looked up with a blank, bewildered look, as if he was seeing ghosts. And then, recognition spread across his face with an almost idiotic expression.

"Devadas, Fred, we've lost everything, and it's all my fault," and he began to weep silently.

Devadas drew near and took his hand. "You have to get up. We aren't safe. What if this part of the trail lets go?"

With the boy's words of encouragement, Lee slowly arose, and the three of them proceeded cautiously back down the trail.

As they cheerlessly headed back toward their last night's camp, there came another aftershock. As Lee had told them, they were not prepared, and their hearts pounded as the ground shook. The aftershocks only lasted for a few seconds or minutes, but they seemed to last an eternity, completely maddening for their duration.

Chapter 13

WHAT NOW?

They were back at the campsite by mid-afternoon. It was a rather sad homecoming. All they had left was a large, heavy yak hair tent containing some charred furniture and a stove, plus what they had been carrying in their day bags or in their hands – their jackets, ponchos, Fred's cameras, Devadas' sketch book, and two trail bars that Devadas had squirreled away in case he got hungry.

Again regrets flooded Lee's mind.

"If only . . . ."   He shook his head with incredulity and began again.

"This part of China has received a major earthquake. We've lost nearly all our gear and all our food, and getting help from anyone is most unlikely, for nobody but Huan even knows where we are. We are miles from farms and villages, and we have no idea about how the farms and villages have fared. We have no food and no expectation of receiving aid. Based on obvious circumstances we are in deep trouble."

"If we hike out, we could manage without the tent as long as it doesn't rain or turn cold and snow. If either of these happens, our situation would become very precarious. Remember our elevation. We've had excellent weather, but we can't depend on it. We have a supply of charcoal in the tent and the stove, so, if we had any food, we could manage for a few nights. If we stay here, we will likely starve and perhaps even freeze to death. We are in a near-alpine environment and they are notable for their harshness. We must ask God for wisdom if we are to survive."

Because they were in no immediate danger, Fred's reaction was cynical.

"How can prayer help? We prayed on the trail, and now all our food, gear, and clothing is gone, and our trek is ruined. If that was an answer to prayer, I'm not sure I want any more divine help."

Devadas piped up, "Why not? We're alive. We have nothing to lose and everything to gain by asking God for help. Besides, maybe our situation is exactly what we need. In many ways, I see this as an expedition into His presence.

Devadas had been processing all that had been happening. There were things going on in his life that defied logic, and this was more of the same. He had seen evil. He had experienced a direct encounter with darkness, and it had frightened him beyond imagination, for it had even put a claim on his life. Yet, there were other events that quietly were revealing something quite different. Circumstances were moving him away from that darkness and toward the light. Why did that Bible scrap appear in the shrubbery? Why had his adopted mother reacted so strangely to his questions about God, the Bible, and Christ? And now, he was isolated in China through the strangest of circumstances, without distractions and with a new friend who was a Christian. How coincidental could that be? There had to be an explanation. Was he in the center of some kind of cosmic battle?

While Fred looked on, Lee and Devadas fell to their knees, and prayed – fervently – for help and deliverance.

Lee concluded their prayer with the words, "Lord God! Help me. I feel terrible, for I am to blame for this predicament. Give me – us – wisdom about what to do."

And then, another aftershocks hit. This one was quite violent.

Fred cried out, "I hate this. I don't think I can take it anymore. We must get away from this place."

Lee stood up, placed his hand on Fred's shoulder, and said, "Where will we go? I'm helpless. Devad can't help you. Qiaowa is six hours by horseback and nine hours for somebody acclimated to the elevation. It would take you or Devadas probably twelve or fourteen hours to get there, and then, what would you find? We don't know, but there may be thousands dead after an earthquake of the size we had."

Fred let out a deep sigh, relieved that all was normal once again.

"I know you are right. There really isn't anything we can. . . . ."

Devadas interrupted, saying, "Maybe we can find some edible wild plants?"

Fred brightened at the prospect.

"Well, that's a possibility. Maybe we could, though I've never been into the 'Euell Gibbons' thing, like finding and eating wild edible plants, and we aren't in the U.S. – we are in China, and I am quite unfamiliar with the vegetation we find here."

Lee added, "My engineering background won't do much good either. We need local help."

Fred looked perplexed.

"The only wild plants I know that can be eaten are ferns. When they are in the fiddlehead stage, 'they are like asparagus, but they aren't good after they have matured. Ferns freeze and die back in the winter, so the season for fiddleheads is past. We might find some that haven't matured too far, but I don't know. Bracken Ferns are edible, but contain carcinogens and shouldn't be eaten. The only safe ones I know are the Cinnamon Fern and the Ostrich Fern. Do any of these grow here? I have no idea. I've heard that horsetails can be eaten if boiled for ten minutes to destroy toxins. In my opinion, we will get really hungry if we are going to try to live off wild plants."

"Well, let's see if we can find some fiddleheads," said Devadas who was getting seriously hungry.

"I think we should wait until morning," said Lee. "It is late, and we need to be thinking about how we are going to spend the night. We need to gather some boughs to put on the ground to protect us from dampness, and we probably should sleep in the tent so we won't get wet from the dew. And, speaking of dew, we better get busy before it falls this evening."

They spent the better part of an hour gathering boughs. On top of these they stretched out their ponchos. They would have to sleep in their clothes with just their jackets for warmth. They had a few days of charcoal left, and the odd round stove was used for cooking, not for heat. Even their few meager creature comforts would be used up quickly – the charcoal and Devadas' sketch book would be used for fire starter, and even Fred's lighter had a limited lifespan.

The only commodity in abundance was drinking water, for the spring was nearby, but their situation did not look promising.

Devadas, by this time, was really hungry. The others were hungry as well, although they didn't talk about it, so Devad suggested they share one of his two energy bars. Eating the sweet cereal, fruit and oil bar didn't satisfy even for a moment. It was just enough to energize their gastric juices.

After getting things ready for the night, they gathered wood so they could light a fire before turning in. Lee had discouraged fires on his previous treks, so the area provided ample dead wood including birch, with bark they were able to use to start the fire rather than sacrificing Devad's sketch book. The fire took some effort to start, but, once going, burned with snap-crackling enthusiasm. Its warmth and brightness warmed their spirits which helped allay their empty and growling stomachs.

The conversation as they sat around the fire began with their risky situation. Had it not been for the earthquake, they would have been somewhere well on their way to Zhongdian. On the bright side they weren't lost, but the earthquake made their situation perilous. Such a disaster usually destroyed the infrastructure of a region. In many ways they were probably better off than if they had been in a town and city. In cities thousands might be homeless, services destroyed, and multitudes more might be dead. The question remained – what should they do.

They lingered around the fire until late. Devadas wanted to know about Lee's faith and asked him many questions about what it meant to be a Christian. Even Fred got drawn into the conversation. He wasn't nearly so cynical as he had been earlier in the day. Fred's problem was his worldview. Evolution answered his needs. To him it was an adequate explanation of why life exists.

Then Fred said, "Devad! Why don't you tell Lee about your dream? Maybe he can help you understand what it means."

He turned to Lee.

"Devad had this dream; well, that's what I would call it. Everybody in the Castle was talking about it. I live in a cottage on the property, so I only know what others told me."

In the flickering light and shadows of the fire, Lee turned toward Fred and asked quizzically, "Castle? Dream? Whatever are you talking about?"

Fred grinned and grunted a short laugh.

"I call the mansion on the estate where we live the Castle. Years ago, the estate was named The Planes because of the large number of sycamore trees on the property – sycamore trees are sometimes called Plane trees. Anyway, I am in charge of the grounds – the 'resident botanist' is my title – and Devadas lives with his adopted mother in the mansion. Actually, the estate is impressive, and the mansion is huge. I have no idea how many rooms it has – if that is a fair assessment of size."

Devad chimed in, "It has sixty-three rooms, not counting the servant's quarters."

"Oh! That is a castle," said Lee, awed by his mental picture of a Chinese palace. "Now, explain about Devad's dream, and, by the way, the name Devadas is a very odd name. Where did it come from?"

Now it was Devadas' turn to talk.

"The dream happened almost two weeks after Fred first told me about his trek idea. The whole thing is still sharp in my mind – when I think about it –which I try not to do."

Lee interjected, "If telling it is too uncomfortable, I don't need . . . ,"

Devadas quickly protested, "Oh, I want to tell you. It may make sense to you, because I . . . . I can't make much sense of it at all – only that it was evil.

"I remember it exactly. Sometime during the middle of the night, I was asleep, and I dreamt or awakened to some dark creatures or figures that descended on me from all directions. As they drew closer, they appeared to be something like men, but not really. And with the figures came terrible noises, rattling or clattering sounds, like the sound of rats scurrying on a metal roof, and, then, these creatures closed in until they were all around me. One of the figures, apparently the one in charge, moved close, and I could almost feel his breath. The apparition wasn't ugly, but was detestable and looked familiar, like I had seen him somewhere before.

"I seemed to be lying in a box looking up into that face of sinister possession and evil control, and the face said, 'Nobody wanted you, but now you are mine. You will serve me and me only. I have plans for you.'"

At that Devadas shuddered and became suddenly cold.

In the firelight Lee's eyes were dark and unfathomable. He was quiet. Nobody said anything. It was as if they had all forgotten where they were and how hungry they were.

After a long while, Lee finally spoke. "Fred referred to your mother as your adopted mother. Do you know your birth mother? Where did you come from? How did you get to – what was it called?"

And Fred and Devadas both said together, "The Planes."

"Yes, The Planes. How was it that you arrived at The Planes?"

Devadas answered, "My friend Hannah said I was left on the doorstep."

Fred said, "I don't know whether I should tell you this in Devadas' presence. What Hannah said . . . Hannah is one of Lady Ellen Smyth's maids and was present when Devadas arrived. I was not. I was in my cottage listening to jazz on my stereo and reading a book, but John Hodge the butler told me all about it later.

"A man in a big car arrived one afternoon. Ellen Smyth must have known him, for John said they spoke on familiar, though not necessarily cordial, terms. John was instructed to get a cardboard carton from the trunk, which he did. He said that what was in the box sickened him, for it was a newborn lying in its own afterbirth. When John lifted the box, the baby let out a cry. Hannah quickly lifted the baby from the box and took it into the house to clean and feed it.

"John said he was told to dispose of the box and afterbirth in the incinerator. Apparently, while he was doing this odious chore, Lady Smyth was told that she was to adopt the baby and even told what to name it. John thought he heard the stranger tell her that he had plans for the child. The stranger then hurriedly drove away."

Devadas' eyes had grown large during this story he had never heard. The stark description of the one who had brought him once again gave him chills.

Lee again was silent, lost in thought.

"It is obvious that you had been abandoned," said Lee, "and that this individual, or man, or whatever he was, had found you. Furthermore, he must hold some control on your adopted mother. She must have been picked because of her wealth. I wonder why?"

And again he was thoughtful.

Fred said, "Lady Smyth was instructed to provide Devad with an education. There is a suite of rooms at The Planes that has become the classroom area. Devad's education has been very structured, with intense classes for ten weeks and then a time of travel. It's a good thing Devad is intelligent because a lesser kid would never have made it. How many languages do you know or speak?"

Devad answered, "Let's see, English, Latin (well I don't speak Latin, but I am able to read and write it), Greek, Arabic, I can get along in Spanish, and do well in French, and German, and am passable in Italian."

At this Lee's eyes grew large. "And how old are you?"

"Fourteen."

Lee asked, "How is it that you learned Arabic? That just doesn't fit with the others. I can understand Latin and Greek, but Arabic?"

"Ms. Borhan wanted me to learn about the development of Western thought and culture. To do that, we studied the cradle of the Western civilization, which she claimed to have originated around the Mediterranean and the Middle East. We first studied the Ancient Greeks, and their roots and the impact they had upon the world. We followed that with the Roman Empire, its ascent and descent. Then we studied the origin and growth of Islam. That is why I was taught Arabic."

"That is curious. I wonder why she didn't have you learn Hebrew as well. Christianity had its origin in the same area," said Lee, "and long before Islam," thinking out loud.

"That first teacher was a doozy," interjected Fred. "She was definitely odd. She sounded like a woman, but was built and dressed more like a man – a big man. I sure wouldn't have wanted to tangle with her."

Devadas said, "I was afraid of her at first, but I guess she was all right. She was nice to me."

"But you didn't say anything about Christianity. Christianity was key to Western Civilization," persisted Lee.

"She hated the Jews and Christians," said Devad. "Once she swore when I once asked her what the Passover was."

"Well, that helps explain why Christianity was not included. Was your teacher an American?" asked Lee.

"I don't know. She might have been, but I know she was born in Iran," answered the boy.

"And she isn't your teacher now?" Lee continued.

"No sir! She left suddenly after I questioned an inconsistency in the Koran," replied Devad.

Fred found Lee's questioning very insightful. He, too, had many questions about Devadas but never pursued them. He was content to have the boy as a friend and Devad's past was none of his business. He liked the boy and enjoyed his company, but Lee's questioning and Devad's answers were adding up to something quite different than simply the life of a very bright young man.

Lee had gotten up to get a couple more pieces of firewood. His mind was a whirl of interest in this youngster, who, but a dozen or so hours ago, was simply a client of his trekking service. Devadas' story was a window into the spiritual battle besetting mankind, and Lee sensed that he might be able to help the boy see his experiences in their rightful context.

After Lee had stirred up the fire, he began again by saying, "I hope you don't mind my questions, for I would like to ask you a few more."

"Sure," said Devad.

"Well, if an Iranian lady was your first teacher, was anybody sent to replace her when she left?"

"Dr. Gustafson took her place," replied Devad.

"What's he like?" said Lee.

"Oh, I like him. We have lots of good discussions. I frustrate him because he can't answer some of my questions."

"Interesting! What kinds of questions do you ask him?" continued Lee.

This remark was all Devadas needed, and he enthusiastically began, "Oh, questions about origins, life, earth, the solar system, space, the 'big bang,' and things related. Science is a way of looking at things of the physical and biological world. It is a method used to explain the environment we live in. I think we treat science as an end in itself, the 'everything,' 'the ultimate,' and it isn't. If you are playing a sonata on the piano, you don't do it with a paintbrush. Science is a tool – and should be used like one.

He continued, "Science doesn't explain truth. That isn't its purpose. It is amoral. And I understand a lot of science – how quantum mechanics explains things on the atomic level, some of what string theory is attempting to explain and a lot more – but these are descriptions or best guesses, based on current evidence. These theories aren't attempting to explain the origins of anything, only how they work.

"One day when I was asking Dr. Gustafson about some inconsistency in regard to evolution, he got frustrated and fired at me, 'Some things you have to accept by faith.' From my reading evolution makes all kinds of assumptions based on what they hope to find someday and on future evidence yet to be discovered. Biological evidence for evolution is sparse at best and becoming more inconsistent with the results coming from research. The genome project shows relationships but does not address origins. And he tells me to take these assumptions on faith. We got into a hot discussion on that one. He thinks religion and faith are for the weak, sort of an intellectual crutch.

"And that reminds me of the time he was explaining that science was only for those things that could be measured, so religious things were off limits, which definitely ruled out explanations that include God such as creation and intelligent design. I asked him something like, 'If God is infinite, how can we as finite beings measure or test him? The finite can only examine the finite, so maybe all that science does in pursuing its goals is to probe the margins of the infinite.'"

Fred saw the logic in what Devadas was saying. "Fourteen years old," he thought, "and this boy has more knowledge and understanding than anyone I've ever heard."

Lee poked at the dwindling fire, and sparks rose toward the night sky, carried by the warmed air. His next question caught both of the others off guard.

"So what do you think about Jesus?"

Fred started to answer, "Well! I guess he was a great man...."

But Lee interrupted, "No, No, No! I agree that what Devadas has said is dead right. But it doesn't address the real issue. What you think of Jesus has implications that go far beyond what Devad would call 'the time-space continuum.' What we think of Jesus is our link to eternity, to the infinite Creator God."

It was Devadas' turn to comment. "I have been reading the New Testament. It says that Jesus is the Son of God. Furthermore, it says that Jesus was...."

And at that moment, another aftershock occurred. This one lasted perhaps two minutes.

But Devadas was not to be deterred. "It says that Jesus was sent to die in our place."

Lee continued from that point. "Man has a wicked nature, and God cannot condone evil. Evil is totally contrary to everything that God is. The only just penalty for evil is death, so God sent his Son to earth to die in our place. Because God is more powerful than death, he was resurrected – rose from the dead – and, with that, did two things. He paid the penalty for man's sin and defeated death. After that he returned to his Father in heaven. When he had gone to his Father, he sent his Spirit to live in us as evidence of that change and to enable us to live holy, righteous lives.

"One of the most familiar verses in the Bible is John 3:16 which says: 'For God so loved the world that he gave his only begotten Son, that whoever believes in him should not perish but have everlasting life.' It is on the one hand so very simple, but on the other so serious, complex, and life altering, it defies description and common sense."

Devadas said quietly, "I believe. Oh Lord God, I believe," and put his head between his knees and sobbed tears of joy.

By this time the fire had become only embers, and Fred's head could be seen nodding his assent against a starry Chinese sky.

"Me too," he said. "I've been such a stubborn ass. I remember that verse from years ago when I was in Sunday school."

With that Fred began to weep.

"Jesus, forgive me for my hard-heartedness. Oh Jesus, cleanse me and make me yours, like your servant Lee."

And with that he cried great tears of repentance and relief.

Lee moved behind them, knelt, and, putting his arms around their shoulders, he prayed:

"Oh Lord God, I thank you for your incredible love and forgiveness. Energize your new servants to be faithful to you. It isn't going to be easy. And God, we need your help. Show us what we should do!"

༄

Daylight was slow in coming. When they woke, the sky was gray, the air was still, and it was unusually quiet. No birds were heard. The weather had been splendid, with pleasant temperatures and mostly clear skies. But now the air around them was pregnant with change, ominous change. As they rose and put on their boots, Lee was the first to speak.

"I don't like the looks of the weather. I think we are in for something, rain for sure and maybe snow. We must move on; we can't stay here. We have no food and only limited shelter."

Fred suggested, "If we are going to move on with the weather turning against us, I think we should use the tent and ropes to create bed rolls and makeshift backpacks."

"An excellent idea," agreed Lee.

So, the three of them proceeded to dismantle the yak-hair tent in preparation for their journey, wherever that might take them. As they worked, they talked about their decisions made by the campfire the previous evening.

Fred admitted, "I've been so pig-headed. I can't believe I refused to accept what was so obvious. I'm going to need a lot of help in this commitment and new life."

Devad agreed, "It makes much sense – at least based on all that I have seen and experienced. It's an obvious conclusion to a lot of evidence. But it sure wasn't what I was taught by my teachers or mother, for that matter. I feel like a huge black cloud has been lifted, and the bright sun has replaced it.

Then he added, "And, I am hungry. Let's eat that last trail bar after we are done and before we set out."

When they finished, they sized up what had been accomplished and concluded that it was the best they could do. They then divided the last trial bar and said a brief prayer of thanksgiving, asking for guidance and protection.

Their decision on which way to proceed had been decided for them, for the high ridge between them and Qiaowa was exposed and well above tree line, and, even without snow, would be buffeted by wind and rain. But with snow, they would be exposed to hypothermia and possible death. Thus, the logical recourse was to move down the valley, hoping to find both food and shelter.

Though sparsely populated, this part of China was not like the mountainous west of the United States. There were people who had lived in the area for generations and eked out a living on small patches of rocky soil. Chinese people were very hospitable and especially considerate to those in need, so the prospects of finding help seemed a good possibility. The only unknown was what the earthquake might have done to the area, and this included the trails as well as damage to homes or villages.

Lee admitted that he had never gone the direction that they were now headed. He said that sooner or later, in going down the valley, they would come to a trail, and he was right. At first it was more like an animal path, for it would continue for a while, then disappear and later pick up again.

After they had walked a while, the trio heard the sound of running water. They were nearing a stream. As the trekkers drew closer, they found a path that showed use and they stopped to drink at the stream. All knew they might pick up giardia or some other parasite, but they had no choice. They needed the water.

After walking for several hours it began to rain, lightly at first. They put on their ponchos, which at first protected them reasonably well. But the light rain turned to a steady down pour, and ponchos won't keep you dry in heavy rain. Now they wet as well as hungry. There was no incentive to stop, for that would only prolong their discomfort.

They were miserable.

Devadas suddenly was inspired to begin singing.

> "I love to go a-wandering,
> Along the mountain track,
> And as I go, I love to sing,
> My knapsack on my back.
> Val-deri, Val-dera,
> Val-deri, Val-dera-ha-ha-ha-ha-ha,
> Val-deri, Val-dera.
> My knapsack on my back."

As he lifted his voice in song, his spirits began to rise. Fred joined him on the second verse, for he had learned the song years before when in scouting.

It was totally unfamiliar to Lee, but he caught on quickly and joined his baritone voice to those of the others.

> "I love to wander by the stream,
> That dances in the sun,
> So joyously it calls to me,
> "Come! Join my happy song!"
> Val-deri, Val-dera,
> Val-deri, Val-dera-ha-ha-ha-ha-ha,
> Val-deri, Val-dera.
> My knapsack on my back.
> "I wave my hat to all I meet,
> And they wave back to me,
> And blackbirds call so loud and sweet,
> From ev'ry green wood tree.
> Val-deri, Val-dera,
> Val-deri, Val-dera-ha-ha-ha-ha-ha,
> Val-deri, Val-dera.
> My knapsack on my back.
> "High overhead, the skylarks wing,
> They never rest at home.
> But just like me, they love to sing,
> As o'er the world we roam.
> Val-deri, Val-dera,
> Val-deri, Val-dera-ha-ha-ha-ha-ha,
> Val-deri, Val-dera.
> My knapsack on my back.

Neill Nutter

> "Oh, may I go a-wandering,
> Until the day I die!
> Oh, may I always laugh and sing,
> Beneath God's clear blue sky!
> Val-deri, Val-dera,
> Val-deri, Val-dera-ha-ha-ha-ha-ha,
> Val-deri, Val-dera.
> My knapsack on my back."

After they had sung 'The Happy Wanderer' a few times, Devadas called out, "Lee, teach us one of your hiking songs!"

Lee replied, "I'm sorry. I don't know any."

"O.K. Fred, how about you?"

Fred came back, "I remember 'Waltzing Matilda.' Do you know that one, Devad?"

"No! How does it go?" was his reply.

And Fred began:

> "Once a jolly swagman camped by a billabong,
> Under the shade of a coolibah tree,
> And he sang as he watched and waited 'til his billy boiled,
> You'll come a-Waltzing Matilda, with me.
> Waltzing Matilda, Waltzing Matilda.
> You'll come a-Waltzing Matilda, with me.
> And he sang as he watched and waited 'til his billy boiled,
> You'll come a-Waltzing Matilda, with me."

"I like it," said Devadas. "Are there any more verses?"

"A few more." And Fred began the next verse.

> "Down came a jumbuck to drink at the billabong,
> Up jumped the swagman and grabbed him with glee,
> And he sang as he stowed that jumbuck in his tucker bag,
> You'll come a-Waltzing Matilda, with me.
> Waltzing Matilda, Waltzing Matilda,
> You'll come a-Waltzing Matilda, with me.
> And he sang as he watched and waited 'til his billy boiled,
> You'll come a-Waltzing Matilda, with me.
> "Down came the squatter, mounted on his thoroughbred,
> Down came the troopers, one, two, three,
> Where's that jolly jumbuck you've got in your tucker bag?
> You'll come a-Waltzing Matilda, with me.
> Waltzing Matilda, Waltzing Matilda,

You'll come a-Waltzing Matilda, with me.
And he sang as he watched and waited 'til his billy boiled,
You'll come a-Waltzing Matilda, with me.
"Up jumped the swagman and sprang into the billabong,
You'll never catch me alive, said he,
And his ghost may be heard as you pass by that billabong,
You'll come a-Waltzing Matilda, with me.
Waltzing Matilda, Waltzing Matilda,
You'll come a-Waltzing Matilda, with me.
And he sang as he watched and waited 'til his billy boiled,
You'll come a-Waltzing Matilda, with me."

Again, Lee was quick to add his baritone to the singing. After repeating the song until they all were hoarse, they were silent, once again remembering their plight. All that could be heard was the sounds of falling rain and the sloshing of their now soaked hiking boots.

After a while, Devadas in a dejected voice said, "I'm hungry and I'm tired."

Fred responded, "You think you're the Lone Ranger?"

Lee called out, "Lone Ranger? Who's that?"

"The Lone Ranger was the hero of an old radio drama that later played on television. He wore a black mask to protect his real identity and went around helping people and saving them from harm. He often traveled alone, hence his name, though he had an Indian companion named Tonto who was an American Indian, not from the continent of India."

"Thanks!" replied Lee.

By this time it was raining harder than ever, and the creek that the trail followed was rising, roily and menacing.

Devadas called out, "I'm really getting cold as well as hungry. We need to find some way to get shelter."

Fred answered, his teeth chattering, "Me too, but where? We haven't seen any signs of civilization, just the woods, stream and trail."

There was nothing to do but trudge on. Even when there was an opening in the forest, they could see nothing. The sky was becoming gloomier, and the rain seemed even to increase in intensity.

Devadas called out to Lee, "Lee! Don't you think we should pray? I'm scared. The weather is becoming frightening, almost like the dream I had."

Lee called back, "Let's do it! You start. We'll pray as we walk."

Devadas prayed, "God! I'm cold, wet, and hungry. It's raining harder. The stream is almost over its banks. I'm scared. Please help us."

And Fred added, "God, I'm kind of new at this, but we are really in trouble. Help us! We really need your help."

"Amen! We definitely needed to pray." Then Lee added, "Just talking to God brings comfort to me."

Then he stopped suddenly, turned around and said, "Wait a minute."

As they caught up with him he said, "We must remember that God is faithful. Even when things seem the darkest, he is always with us. I doubt if you know the 23rd Psalm, but listen to it:

> "The Lord is my Shepherd; I shall not have need. He makes me lie down in green pastures. He leads me beside the calm water. He restores my soul: He leads me in the paths of righteousness for the sake of His name. Even though I walk through the valley of the shadow of death, I will fear no evil: For you are with me. Your rod and your staff comfort me. You even prepare a table before me in the presence of my enemies; You anoint my head with oil; My cup is full and running over. I am certain that goodness and mercy shall follow me all the days of my life and I will dwell in the House of the Lord forever."

"These words comfort me and I hope they comfort you."

And Lee continued, "As we have been walking, I have been convicted of my doubt, fear and remorse. I'm such a slow learner. God tells us that 'all things work together for good to them that love Him.' And I don't act like I believe it. We must remember. God said, 'Be strong and of good courage.' For all we know, help may be right around the next bend in the trail."

Chapter 14
Real Enlightenment

They hadn't gone more thirty or forty yards when the trail turned into an open area, and ahead on a hill was a brightly painted building, somewhat reminiscent of what they had seen in Tibet. It had three floors, and the roof had wide overhangs. Light was shining from the windows on the second floor. Lee, who was leading the way, paused. The others caught up with him, and they stood looking at it in kind of a stupor.

"It's a temple," said Lee.

It wasn't destroyed by the earthquake," added Fred.

"Our prayers are answered," cried Devadas.

"So soon!" Lee said softly.

And with that, they hurried forward to the path that led to the door of the temple.

Not intending to, but with their relief and enthusiasm, they pounded on the door. A short moment later, a monk opened it and, with a big smile, bid them come in out of the rain.

Lee began in Chinese. "We seek food and . . ."

The monk waved his request aside and answered Lee in what Fred and Devadas heard as perfect English, "We have been expecting you. You are all soaking wet. Follow me."

He led them to a warm room where towels and dry clothes were laid out in expectation of their arrival.

"Change your clothes. Dry yourselves off, and put your wet clothes in the hamper," he pointed to a large woven basket, "and I will come for you in about fifteen minutes to take you to your dinner."

As the monk left the room and closed the door, Devadas, Fred and Lee looked at one another in astonishment. In a moment they all began hurriedly to strip, dry themselves, and put on the clothes left for them. The clothes themselves were a surprise, for they were more western in style and were properly sized for each. It felt so good to be warm and dry in clean clothes. They were given slippers rather than shoes to put on.

Almost as soon as they were ready, the monk came for them with a warm smile and said, "Now it is time that you are fed. You haven't eaten anything other than two trail bars in the last twenty-four hours. You must be starved."

As they followed the monk, they looked at each other, mouths agape and wondering at his knowledge. In moments they came to a large dining room containing a long table covered by cloths with two large steaming tureens containing something that smelled delicious and a steaming pot of what they assumed was tea. There were chairs placed around the table, and the monk motioned for them to take their places.

"We are thrilled to have such distinguished guests share our humble fare."

Devadas started to ask the monk a question. Again the monk waved the question aside and said, "Eat now, we will talk later."

So the visitors sat down and two younger monks took bowls and cups, filled them and brought them to the guests.

"Eat and enjoy. We have plenty."

Devadas, Fred and Lee did not have to be asked a second time, but as Fred and Devadas began to lift their filled spoons, Lee stopped them.

"Our prayers were answered above and beyond what we hoped or imagined. We must pray."

With that, Lee simply said, "Thank you, God, for answering our prayers and for this food."

And all said, "Amen!"

The monk's eyes glistened, his smile grew larger, and he watched with pleasure as his guests enjoyed the food.

When they had eaten their fill, Devadas said, "I don't know what it was, but I've never eaten anything that tasted so good." The others nodded their heads vigorously in agreement.

Their host, still smiling, replied, "Hunger is the perfect garnish for humble food. Kings seldom, if ever, have that delight.

"Come, now is the time for talk. Please follow me."

He led them to a large colorful yet cozy room with couches that faced an open fire. The monk bid them find a comfortable seat and sat down himself.

"Now," he said, "introduce yourselves. To have such distinguished guests is a great honor to our humble temple. Who are you, and why have you come?"

Devadas quickly said, "My name is Devadas Smyth. This is Lee, and this is Fred Riley," as he pointed to his friends. "Fred and I were on a trek, and Lee is our guide. After the earthquake, our horses fell off the trail with all our gear."

"Ah, the earthquake? What a violent one it was, but, strangely, our humble temple was spared all but minor damage. Now, let us talk about you. Aren't you all 'Enlightened Ones?' I really don't understand this at all. Two of you are English, and Lee is Lisu, yet you come to our humble temple speaking fluent Tibetan, my native tongue. I don't understand this at all."

At this the travelers turned to one-another, dumbfounded. They spoke together, " We are speaking Tibetan? Enlightened ones?"

And they looked at one another, astonished that these monks heard them speaking Tibetan.

Devadas said, "And we are hearing them speak in American English."

Lee responded, "And I hear them in Lisu."

Devadas began to understand a little of what was happening, and he turned quizzically to the monk and asked, "How did you know we were coming? What caused you to expect us?"

Their host replied, "Early today, I was doing my morning prayers, and I had a vision – my first. In it I saw a man in a shimmering white robe who spoke with a voice like thunder, unlike anything I had ever heard. He said, 'A young man whom I have chosen for good works is pursued by the evil one called Death. He is accompanied by two of my faithful servants. Care well for them.'"

"How did you know the sizes of our clothes?" asked Fred.

"That I cannot answer," replied the monk." Now, let me ask you some questions, if I may."

"Go ahead," replied the three.

"You don't speak Tibetan?" he asked.

"I do a little," answered Lee, "but neither Fred nor Devadas do."

The monk shook his head and asked, "Then what language are you speaking?"

Devad said, "American English."

"Amazing," said the monk, "and what language do you hear me speaking?"

"American," said Devadas.

"Lisu," added Lee.

"I don't understand this at all," replied their host.

"Nor do we," added Fred.

The monk looked pensive. "Who was that man in the shimmering white robe?"

Lee said quietly, "I believe it was Jesus Christ."

"Jesus Christ? I thought he was one who lived long ago and was just another prophet or enlightened one." He paused a moment, thinking about the implication of his vision, and then went on, "If he spoke to me, he is alive. If he is alive, he was resurrected. If he was resurrected, then the Christian's God is 'the one true God,' and I have been deluded all these years."

Again, there was a long pause as he looked down at his feet, and then at Lee, Fred, and Devadas. "Are you gods?" he asked the three. "The vision implied that the young man is special. Are you a god?" he asked Devadas directly.

"No!" answered Devadas, humbly, "I'm just a servant of Jesus, desiring to do the will of God as it would seem you are."

"But, I'm full of sin, full of desire, and all my penance and efforts have accomplished nothing. Why would I be chosen to see Jesus – who do you say he is – the Son of God? What must I do to be saved?" he frantically asked and stood, his hands open expectantly.

"Humble yourself before God. Repent! Admit your sins, and tell him that you accept his free gift of salvation, the God-man Christ Jesus. God's word says; God loved the world so much that he gave his only son, that whoever believes in him should not perish but have everlasting life!" said Lee.

"Oh, I believe! I have seen him and heard his voice. I believe!" And with that, the monk fell to his knees in a prayer of penance and thanksgiving.

Lee whispered to Devadas, "Go down where we are staying, and get my Bible. Fred and I will stay here and pray with him."

Both Lee and Fred knelt beside the monk, praising God for the miracle of new birth.

In just minutes Devadas was back with the Chinese Bible. Lee had wrapped it in plastic so it wouldn't get wet. Devad handed it to Lee, and then he, too, knelt and prayed.

When the monk had finished, they all stood. Lee gave him his Bible and said, "These are the words of life: God's Holy Word, the Bible. It is in Chinese. Can you read it?"

At the monk's nod of assent, Lee continued, "You have begun a journey. This is your guidebook. Study it, feed on it. In it is the Truth of God."

Twice Chosen

That evening, they talked with the monk and his novitiates until late into the night. Discussion about the senior, most respected monk converting to Christianity – accepting Christ – proved to be very lively. Several of the younger monks were fascinated by their respected elder's change and asked many questions, while others were filled with skepticism and even anger about his renunciation of Buddhism, their life belief. Those that would not believe refused to listen further and left the room, voices raised in anger.

The old monk explained to those who remained that the work of Christ was the only solution to accomplishing the demands of the eight-fold path. Nirvana was accessible, but it was through the selflessness of Jesus Christ, not through human effort, that atonement was made, and that all his previous efforts at devotion – the chants, offerings, pilgrimages, mantras, all made to images – should no longer be pursued, for they were of no value.

From now on all his devotion would be to the Creator God who had spoken directly to him and had sent His messengers to enlighten him to the True God. Furthermore, he now possessed the Bible, the guidebook to the true eight-fold path, and they would study the free way to the true nirvana.

Devadas, Fred and Lee spent a night of contented and restful sleep. As they rubbed the sleep from their eyes, the events of the previous day were again brought to mind, and they marveled at God's love, grace, and saving power – a power they saw demonstrated in countless ways.

Before going to the dining room for their morning tea, they concluded they needed to spend some time in prayer before their day was swallowed up with activity. Devadas would pray first, then Fred, and Lee would close.

Devadas began, "Jesus, God! Thank you for protecting us. Thank you for bringing us to China and opening my eyes to who you are. Thank you for sending Lee to be our guide. Little did we know that what we had believed to be only a trek would prove to be a spiritual odyssey. Thank you for rescuing me from the evil one. Oh God! Thank you for your love. Thank you for your protection. Thank you for our new beginning. Oh God! Thank you so much that you love us."

Fred picked up where Devadas had ended.

"God! I can't believe this. It seems like a dream. Thank you for freeing me from the roots of my self-centeredness. Replace the weeds that I've cultivated so carefully with the fruits of your love. Replace my darkness with your light, the light that we need to grow. Help me to absorb your energy, your strength, and power to do good and to love you."

Lee continued, "Thank you, Lord God, for using me to share your incredible love, first with Devadas, Fred, and now these new brothers in Christ. I pray for all of these – but especially these men who have broken with the only faith they have ever known and have embraced you. They will have a difficulty, for they will be hated and, even now, are hated, and there will be those who would kill them. Pour out your divine protection upon them. Fill them with your presence. Encourage them. Help them to quickly learn the truths of your Word.

"Lord, we have a new set of decisions to make. Show us what we should do, where we should go, and when. Nothing has gone like I, like we, expected. We need revelation from you so that we may do what is right for the advancement of your kingdom.

"Thank you, God, for answering our prayers. Amen"

When Lee concluded, they hugged each other and went to the dining room for their breakfast tea.

Most of the monks were gathered around the large pottery teapot where there was a lot activity. Since their cups were small, refills were frequent. As Fred, Devadas and Lee entered the room, attention was drawn to the newcomers. That the perspectives of the young monks were polarized was obvious. Dialogue was thick. There were questions about Christ and Christianity. There was vigorous discussion about the pros and cons of Buddhism and Christianity. The spirit of the room was lively and exhilarating.

The elder monk approached Lee and asked, "When are you planning to leave and when will you return? We have been so blessed by your presence. Everything is changed. There is an energy here now that was never here before. Before, there was tranquility, for that is what every good Buddhist strives for – right speech, right behavior, right effort – but it was a forced harmony. Today, things are not tranquil, some of the young men are exuberant in their joy, others demand further explanation. It is a wonderful miracle." His questions and comments tumbled from his lips so rapidly, Lee could not answer.

"To answer your questions – when will we leave, and when will we return – I can't tell you. The Americans have their return flights previously booked. I am not sure when that is, but it surely can't be more than a week from now, and it may not be that long."

"Other than caring for their needs, I don't have a schedule. Oddly, I do not have another trekking tour scheduled for nearly three weeks. Why do you ask?"

Lee cocked his head to one side as if to emphasize his curiosity.

The monk replied, "It would be so good if you could stay with us and teach us from God's guide to the eight-fold path. We have so much to learn of God and his Son Jesus. We all discussed this hope before you came in for tea."

Twice Chosen

Lee looked thoughtful. "I have to get my friends to Zhongdian in order for them to fly to Beijing and then back to the U.S. My jeep is in Qiaowa where my assistant Huan lives."

The elder monk rubbed his hands together as he thought. "From here to Zhongdian is a long and complicated journey. Perhaps they could change their flight from Zhongdian to Xichang? To get them to Xichang would not be as difficult. It would require help, but I have help that could assist them to a bus route going to Xichang."

"We'll have to ask them, but I do have both a signed agreement and a moral responsibility to their safety and well being, and have given assurance that they will be safely on the plane to Beijing," added Lee, still unsure of doing what the monk requested. "Let us have 24 hours to consider and pray about your request before giving you an answer if we can take advantage of your generous and kind hospitality for that long."

The monk's broad smile assured Lee that that he approved of this plan as he answered, "Of course," and then his smile became a sly grin as he continued, "if after dinner, you will teach us from God's word."

Lee twisted his mouth and bit on his lip, as he considered the conditions for their staying another 24 hours. Whatever would he teach to these new converts? And, could he persuade the doubters in such a short time and with no preparation? What could he do that would be important for their faith or their lack of faith? It might be the only teaching they would ever receive. As he thought, he prayed earnestly and fervently.

The answer came quickly. He knew what he would do. He would take the Bible he had given to the temple and read aloud from the book of John, opening up the thoughts and ideas presented by John to the monks, and dialoguing with them until they could go no further.

Once God had given him a plan, he spoke again to the elder monk, "I accept your conditions, but I would like to borrow God's Word from you for the evening."

Fred and Devadas had been having a great time of conversation with some of the young monks when Lee approached.

"Let's find a place where we can sit down privately and talk. We need to plan what we are going to do. The time of your flight is rapidly drawing near. We are not anywhere near Zhongdian and are a long way from Xichang, and that city is probably devastated. How we can get you to either, or, more likely, if we can get you to either, is unknown. Added to this, the old monk in charge – the one who had the vision of our arrival – has asked me to stay on and teach them the Scriptures, and, while that has much appeal, I have concerns about my responsibilities to you."

As they moved to an area away from the teapot where they could sit and talk with fewer interruptions, Lee continued, "The way I see all this is, we – you – have several options."

At this Lee shook his head in frustration, disbelief, and uncertainty.

"Number one, we can leave tomorrow morning with directions about how to find the nearest public transportation to Xichang, but we don't know what the conditions are there. Number two, the monks are willing to supply you with someone who will take you to where you can get transportation, and I can stay here. How much time it would take to do either of these is anybody's guess, though the monks would probably have a good idea. Number three, you can stay here with me, but, we have no idea how long God will enable you to communicate with the monks in their native language. I don't think this is a good option, and, besides, you would miss your flight. Lastly, if we could find a phone and that is questionable, we could have Huan bring provisions from Quiowa, if there is anything left, and continue the trek which would require a lengthy detour around that chunk of missing trail. That would make the trip a whole lot more difficult. And with the time already lost, you would definitely miss your flight back to the U.S. In my opinion we really are only left with options one and two."

"God has guided us and answered our prayers. We must pray and trust him on this," added Devadas.

Fred agreed and added, "It is too noisy here, and there are too many people. I say we retreat to our sleeping quarters, so we can pray without being interrupted."

With that he got up and left, and the others followed him.

The three prayed until they began repeating themselves. Their prayers included thanksgiving for the miraculous way they had been cared for, but first and foremost they prayed for God's direction in what they should do now.

When they finished, Devadas was the first to speak. "While praying, I kept getting the strong impression that I need to go home as soon as possible. All that has happened on our trekking has to do with me. Since I began responding to God's love, I am convinced the evil one I saw in my dream is trying to kill me, and, since you are my friends, you are a target of the same hatred. I believe my mother is in danger as well, as are all those at The Planes. It is becoming increasingly clear that I am needed at home. God hasn't finished the work that he has begun in me, and they need me to open their eyes to God's love and truth."

Fred concurred, "What Devad said makes sense. Our journey has become much more than a trekking experience. God is moving, and, while praying, I got the same strong impression – go home and quickly. I don't think we need

Twice Chosen

Lee on this part of the trip. These men here in the temple need the truth of God. Neither Devadas nor I can be of much help, for we are babes in this New Life, and, when God's gift of understanding our new friends leaves us, we will only be in the way. I can help Devad and support him as he reports to his mother and to the staff."

"God has answered our prayer by giving us agreement," added Lee. "I'm confident that you two can get safely to Xichang where you can begin your flight home and I am needed here. The time is short with these men. As soon as the word gets out about the conversion of these living in this temple, there will be intense persecution. The time of teaching is now, and actually begins tonight."

"Tonight?" gasped Devadas, "What do you mean tonight?"

Lee laughingly told them of his earlier conversation with the elder monk and then added, "They are very anxious for the studies to begin, especially the old one. They realize that their hours and days are numbered, at least here, so the lessons begin tonight."

"Great!" said Fred, "Can we listen in?"

"Of course," answered Lee, "and now let's go back and tell the monk what we have decided."

The evening's teaching was spirited and exciting. There were so many questions. Devadas was almost overcome by the spirit that filled the place. It was like nothing he had ever experienced in his studies at home, the many trips taken, and especially the Hajj. There was something electric that was happening. Lee said later that it was the presence of God the Holy Spirit, and he had never experienced anything like it either. Even the remaining unbelievers had yielded their lives to Christ. All Fred could do was shake his head. All except Lee were novice Christians, and they all had the sense that something truly extraordinary was taking place, as if a lifetime of being one of God's children was crammed into one long evening. All were nourished and strengthened by the Spirit of God.

Chapter 15

A Long Journey

The next morning the temple buzzed with activity. Tea had been put on early. Food for a two days' journey was prepared. By lot one of the younger monks had been selected to escort Devadas and Fred to the nearest location where they could get public transportation (a bus) to Xichang. The trip would take them at least two days. The first night they were to stay in a farmer's home, and the next night they would stay in an inn of sorts where they would wait for the bus, whenever it might arrive. There was a bus schedule, but, in the mountains of western China, schedules were an ideal, not necessarily a reality.

Their trek to catch the bus was a long hike but not expected to be arduous, at least in regard to the terrain. It was down a deep, narrow valley with slopes so steep it could rightfully be called a canyon. Sunshine was limited to just a few hours each day. The change in elevation from river to ridge top was measured in thousands of feet. Agriculture here was limited to a terraced patch here or there adjacent to the river. That people could live here at all and eke out any kind of existence was a tribute to the resourcefulness of man.

The trek had not worked out the way they had planed. They had experienced a large earthquake. They had heard and seen the rockslides, destroying the trail. Their horses in great fright had fallen off the trail into the chasm below with their gear. And the rainstorm had forced them to go down into the valley requiring them to seek shelter in the temple rather than try to hike over the ridge to Qiaowa. God works in mysterious ways to accomplish His purposes.

They now saw no evidence of the earthquake they had experienced. The epicenter must have been in the direction from which they had come, but, even though the trail was downhill, the trek out proved to be difficult because the recent heavy rains had washed out a number of bridges.

Some distance downstream was the first washout. The trail crossed the river due to precipitous rock on their side and the bridge across was gone. Because the river narrowed as it passed into the canyon, there was a logjam. Their only recourse was to use the logjam for a bridge, a very risky business. As Devadas considered the crossing, he cried aloud, "Oh God, help us!"

The crossing had a few very tense moments, with one a near calamity. The logs were wet and slippery. Fred and Devadas were wearing their hiking boots and had reasonably good traction, but the young monk did not have that advantage and slipped off a log into the swift and icy cold waters. As he went in, he was able to grab an adjacent snag and hang on long enough for Fred to grip his arm. With the help of Devadas, they were able to get him to safety.

By the time they reached the opposite bank, they were shaking from their close call. Fred had a change of clothes in his makeshift backpack, and their young friend from the temple hastily changed. The young monk was quite a bit smaller than Fred, so the clothes were not a good fit, but they were dry and warm. Their guide cached his wet clothes behind some rocks and marked their location with a cairn, so he could find them on his return trip. After their heart rates had slowed to near normal, they knelt by the river and thanked God for getting them all across safely.

Another close call came later where valley again narrowed. As they were walking through the narrows they met an old Chinese peasant approaching them, and they stopped to ask him about the condition of the trail farther along. Suddenly, without warning, a rock fall came crashing down on the road just ahead where they were going. All were stunned. Again, the three immediately knelt and thanked God before continuing. When they concluded their prayer, the old man was gone, and their hearts were full of wonder as they carefully climbed across the newly fallen rocks covering their way.

It was dusk by the time they reached the location where they would spend the night. It was a low log house, very primitive, in which five people lived: an old man, a younger man and his wife, and two children. To enter required stooping to get through the door. Inside were two rooms, both with dirt floors. One room was open and had a fire burning in the middle of the room. It was their principal living quarters. The other room was presumably where they would sleep. The family used both rooms except when they had guests. In the second room was a pile of yak hides, which would be their bed.

These were the most primitive sleeping conditions they had encountered on their entire trip including Lee's tent, even after the fire.

For supper they had yak butter tea and what they thought to be tsampa. It was edible, probably nourishing, but the taste was not to their liking. When Devadas made a face, Fred said, "Beggars can't be choosers!" The young monk seemed to relish what they ate and smiled his approval.

The hides they slept on must have been home to a colony of fleas, for they woke with many bites where the insects had gotten in their clothes. Besides the fleas they were cold, and may never have made it through the night except for their fleece jackets.

Their breakfast was a repeat of their supper the night before, and it tasted no better then it did then. When they left, they paid the young man for their lodging, and he smiled his thanks through several missing teeth.

The three were not sorry to be on the trail again although their young companion had probably come from such an environment.

The second day of hiking was not nearly as eventful as the first. The trail had become a road and was in relatively good condition. At times the valley opened wide to terraced hillsides with crops, and livestock were often seen. With the openness came wide sweeping vistas and a sky laced with clouds. The river had grown larger, having been fed by numerous rills and streams. Whereas the previous day they felt almost crushed by a gloomy pessimism like the river which was squeezed into its shadowy narrowness, today the expanse of the landscape seemed to lift their spirits with a certain ebullience and freedom.

When they got to the tiny village where they could get the bus to Xichang, it was dusk. Their young friend led them to a restaurant where they could get food before going to the Inn. Their meal consisted of stir-fried ham, green chilies, and potatoes. Devadas and Fred both had Coca-Cola, and the young monk had hot tea.

After completing the meal, they went to the inn where they were shown their room. They then bid goodbye to their companion of the last two days for he would stay with friends.

The innkeeper informed them that he did not know when the bus to Xichang would arrive, for the heavy rains had washed out the road in some places and caused earth and rock slides in others. He said that it usually came in just before dinnertime. One thing they noticed as they talked to the innkeeper. They heard him in broken English, and, as he had some difficulty understanding them, they concluded that the ability to hear and speak in a clear and fluent manner in the native tongue was gone. God had gifted them as long as it was necessary.

The bus did not arrive for over 24 hours. After the driver let his disgruntled passengers embark, he climbed from the bus, and it was clear that his journey had been long and difficult. As he approached the inn, which was the bus stop and the end of the route, the innkeeper went out to meet him. The driver's eyes were baggy and bloodshot, his clothes looked like he had slept in them, and, as he talked, he gestured constantly. He was anything but the typical, inscrutable Oriental. Since the driver only spoke Chinese, and they no longer had the language gift, they had to wait for the innkeeper to tell them in broken English when the bus would return to Xichang and how long the trip might take.

When the driver was finished, Fred asked the innkeeper, "What did he tell you?"

"He said the road is washed out in many places. He was afraid to drive after dark. He said that in places, he and the passengers had to get off to move rocks from their path, and, in others, to fill in gullies in order to continue. Finally, he told his passengers he wasn't going any farther until daylight and took his keys out of the ignition, put his head back, and promptly went to sleep. The passengers were not happy. He said that he will try to return to Xichang in the morning. By then road crews may have worked on the road."

At that the innkeeper turned and went back inside.

Fred turned to Devadas and said, "Well, buddy, I guess we might as well get another night's sleep, because I don't think we are going anywhere until morning."

Fred and Devadas were awake early. They didn't want to miss their ride, for they were anxious to get home. They had no idea what awaited them because their tickets were from Zhongdian to Beijing. They had no idea if they could persuade the airline to exchange their tickets, or if they would have to take the loss and purchase new ones, or even if they could get a flight. At this point cost was not the concern, only getting home to The Planes.

It wasn't until after breakfast that the driver was ready to leave, and, even then, he did not seem to be in a hurry. When they left, there were about a dozen other people who had boarded the bus. There were women with baskets of what appeared to be food, small children, two men, and one very old man. In addition to boxes, bags and produce were loaded in the under-storage. There were also bags of what appeared to be mail. The bus was obviously a lifeline to the rest of the world.

There were few straight stretches of road. In places it seemed that the road went straight up, and the bus groaned along slowly up and over divides. At times it clung to the edges of steep valleys. In others it closely followed rivers. Often the road was above tree line, and on the shady sides of the hills were patches of snow. There was much water running down, over, along, and under the road. The road crew had apparently been out and repaired the worst washouts, but the road was far from smooth. It was hard work for the driver as he was constantly shifting gears to accommodate the vagaries of the geography.

On the heights the views were fantastic with mountain peaks seen in all directions. Occasionally there would be a glimpse of blue where a mountain lake would be seen. The bus made frequent stops to add and drop off its passengers. Sometimes, the driver would get out and open the under-storage to add or remove goods.

Fred dozed, while Devadas gazed out the window, riveted by the scenery. On one uphill stretch the bus sputtered, and died. The driver stopped in the middle of the road, got out, walked around to the back of the bus, and did something to the engine to coax it back to life, and they were off again. There was little traffic, mostly trucks and maintenance vehicles.

As they neared Xichang, they could see no evidence of earthquake damage, and the bus sped up on the now mostly-paved road. They followed a broad floodplain for some time and then went east into the city. The bus station was in the center of the city. There they climbed off, and, taking their daypacks, went to a desk to inquire about getting to the airport. Fortunately, a van was leaving for the airport in only a few minutes, so they only had a short wait.

The trip to the airport seemed to take no time at all. Both Devadas and Fred were fascinated by the activity, the traffic, and the buildings. It was so different from the high ridges, deep valleys, rushing rivers, and the bucolic, even primeval lifestyles they had observed. But, even in those isolated rural areas, there was a yielding to the times, for the people they had met were strangely aware of what was taking place in China and in the rest of the world.

The airport was filled with activity, for Xichang was an economic hub in that section of Sichuan Province. The terminal buzzed with activity.

Fred and Devadas worked their way to the airline desk of the company that had flown them from Beijing to Lhasa, and from Lhasa to Xichang. The young man behind the desk was either uncomfortable with the questions that Fred asked or with trying to explain things in English, so he asked them to wait, and, moments later, returned with a young woman who, apparently briefed by her co-worker, came to the desk, smiled at them, and proceeded to help with their requests.

They were not able to get a refund for their tickets from Zhongdian to Beijing, but she was able to provide them with new tickets from Xichang to Beijing. After checking their flight number on her computer, she said that it should be possible to catch their plane to the States, but, if there were any delays, they might have to take a later flight.

Fred and Devadas looked at each other, nodded their respective heads, and proceeded to make the necessary arrangements for their flight to Beijing.

༄

They had caught their scheduled flight back to the United States. The estimated airtime was about sixteen hours and was non-stop from Beijing to Chicago. The shortest distance would take them along the north edge of the Pacific Ocean, paralleling the Sea of Japan, across the Sea of Okhotsk, over the Kamchatka Peninsula, and almost parallel to the Aleutian Islands before entering Canadian air space. It was night when they left Beijing, and, as they flew east, they quickly were greeted by daylight.

Devadas always wanted a seat by a window, and, since they flew business class, his view was unobstructed by the wings. He was very excited about getting home, though experienced growing apprehension over what would await him. His newfound faith reassured him, but the events of the past ten days – earthquakes, rainstorms, washed-out bridges, rock slides, and the like – gave him pause. He and Fred talked about the events of their trip.

"I'm sure sorry that the trekking didn't work out as planned," said Fred, "especially for you. Don't get me wrong. We saw and did a lot and had a lot more excitement than we had bargained for, but our time in Sichuan Province certainly wasn't what I'd planned."

"Its O.K., Fred. I've been thinking a lot about what happened in the last couple of weeks. I think we've been part of a much bigger drama then we realize. Remember when I told Lee about the dream, and then you gave me some insight into where I came from?"

"How could I forget? That was the night after nearly perishing on the mountainside and losing all our food," mused Fred.

"Well, the way I see it, I was found by something or someone who was very evil, and he brought me to The Planes. Whatever or whoever did that had some kind of hold – like Lee had said – on my mother, and she was pushed into raising me because she had the money and the staff to do it. Whoever it was wanted to use me in some diabolical way if that dream I had was any indication.

"And why was God never mentioned? Oh, I take that back," Devadas continued. "Ms. Borhan almost shoved Allah down my throat. She took me to Israel for my education, but it turned out that was sort of a disguised way of getting me to take the Hajj. What was she trying to accomplish? I think she believed that I might have some religious experience that would move me to believe like she did. She had a totally irrational hatred for the Jews, and that caught my attention. When I asked her about an inconsistency about Islam, she disappeared.

"And then Mr. Gustafson came as her replacement. I like him, but he has really been promoting the concept of atheism. He never refers to it as that, but God has no place in the way he perceives reality. Somehow, I was enabled to recognize that the faith needed to believe what he taught was at least as great or maybe greater than that of believing in a Transcendent Creator."

And then Devadas was quiet, while Fred just sat in his seat looking thoughtful. After a few minutes, Devad continued, "And then there was that scrap of a page from an old Bible caught in the shrubbery."

At that Fred interjected, "That is strange. We have very little litter at The Planes for we have people walking the grounds nearly every day making sure everything is picked up. When there is, it is almost always something from a fast food restaurant, or maybe a piece of plastic. What is really strange is that it came from a Bible."

"Well, it sure got my attention. It was like opening a door to a whole new dimension. And then when asked about it, Eliza gave me her old Bible and commented that the help had all been instructed to have nothing to do with the Bible or religion."

Fred said, "Yeah! I remember what you had said about that."

"But that dream. It was almost a shriek of possession. I don't know which frightened me most, the shapes or the claim on me." He shuddered at the thought and then went on, "There has to be a connection."

Devadas paused again and sat silently, staring straight ahead. Again he began, "And then there was the earthquake. The lamp barely hit me, and the earthquake kept happening – those aftershocks, and then that experience on the trail, and losing the horses and our gear – that was weird."

"Then going down the valley and finding the temple – that was even more strange than the earthquake. We knew their language, or they knew ours – really strange! But we were able to communicate freely – just like we'd been friends forever. And in all that, you, I, the monks, we all believed God. It is all so incredible."

Fred was listening to Devadas reflect on the latter part of the journey, and, at the pause said, "Well, I'm really glad to have been 'born again,' as Jesus explained things to Nicodemus."

Devad said nothing for a very long time. In fact, Fred had taken one of the sales catalogues, always on every flight, and was idly thumbing through it when Devadas spoke again.

"I don't think all of this is over."

"What isn't over?" said Fred as he looked up.

"The attempts to destroy us. God has taken care of us, again and again, and in ways we probably haven't even recognized. I think that we may be in for some more of what we have already encountered – attempts on our lives and God's protection. I suspect it happens all the time, but we just don't see it."

With that he put on his headphones, checked the choices available, lay back in his seat, and began listening to music, savoring what he regarded as one of the great blessing of life.

It was some time into their flight, when the airplane suddenly bounced upward and the hundreds of passengers were all suddenly awake. The cabin lights came on, and the captain's voice came on over the loudspeaker just as the seatbelt sign lit up.

"Please fasten your seat belts. We have run into some strange turbulence. There has been no predicted bad weather. I suspect that the bump just experienced is a thermal updraft from an erupting volcano. We have received no reports of the threat of volcanic eruptions, but I am concerned that this is what has happened for we are flying adjacent to the Aleutian Islands, a long string of volcanoes. We may be in for some very tense moments."

Devadas and Fred looked at each other. Fred was the first to speak.

"I don't like the sounds of this. When volcanic ash gets into a jet engine, it really messes things up."

There was some continued turbulence, and then the plane's motion stabilized, but the seat belt light remained on. Very little time had elapsed when one of the plane's jet engines stopped, and the aircraft began a very slow descent. It seemed only seconds before the second engine cut out. Now, the rate of descent increased. The silence was deafening. Listening carefully, Fred and Devad could hear sobbing. Yet another engine quit, and their rate of descent increased even more rapidly.

The captain's voice was again heard.

"We have serious problems. Remember that life jackets are under your seats. Review the instructions for ditching, landing at sea and putting on the life jackets. If we have to make an ocean landing, it will not be a pretty sight. Make sure the seat backs are in the upright position. I don't know what you believe, but if you have never prayed, this is the time to begin."

Turning toward Fred, Devadas said, "I knew it! What is happening is because of us – because of me. Pray! We have been spared before. Perhaps God will spare us again."

And they prayed.

Because it was daylight, they could now see the ocean much too clearly. Fred said between prayers, "I'm so glad I accepted Jesus."

They probably weren't more than a thousand feet above the ocean's surface when what felt like a mighty hand beneath them stopped the descent, and the engines – first number one, then two, than the third and fourth – caught, and the great plane rose again toward the heavens.

The captain's voice was again heard, "That was close! Too close! Way too close. We don't know what has happened, but all four engines seem to be running fine. Rather than tempt fate, we are going to divert toward Anchorage where we will make an unscheduled landing. If we have no further problems, we should be landing in about three hours."

Devad and Fred bowed their heads in thanksgiving.

"When is this going to end?" thought Devadas to himself.

Chapter 16

HOME AT LAST

After changing planes in Anchorage, the remainder of the flight was without incident.

Nearly all of The Planes staff accompanied Ellen Smyth to the airport to greet the travelers. They were welcomed almost as heroes, for the news regarding the volcanic eruption and near crash in the North Pacific made national TV. When the flight crew was interviewed, they had no explanation for why they had not crashed into the sea, and the FAA and NTSB were meticulously going over everything, looking for an explanation.

All the hugging and kissing embarrassed Devadas, and Fred had never received so much attention. It was a homecoming like you would expect only if you had returned from a war zone after a year or more absence. Everybody was talking at once, asking questions and commenting on how good or how thin the travelers were, or saying, "You need a haircut."

They had rented a stretch limousine so all could ride together, and no one would have to miss anything said, but, because everyone was talking at once, it was doubtful that anyone heard anything. Simms was having a ball as the driver of the monster vehicle, for, with all the cars in The Planes stable, to go outside and rent a limousine was unheard of. They didn't do it because they didn't need to, but this was a special occasion. Of course, this was as long as a school bus and shiny black, nothing like his MG, but it really made him feel important, and very special.

When they arrived at The Planes' Ellen Smyth had everyone assemble in the library. She had considered using the dining room, for a celebration

Neill Nutter

and refreshments were in order, but that was much too formal for such an occasion, and the ballroom was too cavernous. The library was just right for such a joyous gathering. It had enough seating, and there were tables for the refreshments and for displaying the books, magazine, maps, pictures, and anything related to the adventure that Devad and Fred had experienced.

Eliza had baked both of Devadas' favorite cookies for the occasion. His very favorite was chocolate chip cookies without nuts – and preferably with extra chips. He didn't like them crispy, so these were soft and chewy. His next favorite cookies were called molasses krinkles, again soft and chewy, and he liked them sprinkled with red and green colored sugar crystals. Fred's favorite was chocolate chip mint brownies. To be on the safe side, Eliza made several other varieties as well, one of which was her personal favorite, a date nut cookie. She also provided the choice of coffee, tea, hot chocolate, or mulled cider. Lady Smyth had ruled out wine because she felt it wasn't appropriate for a celebration of this sort, though she personally liked wine and had many fine vintage wines available.

Mary Tompkins had set up a video projector to show Fred's pictures, and his digital camera was connected to the projector. The pictures would be unedited, at least for final form. Devadas' sketches were laid out for all to examine at their leisure.

When the pictures were projected, both Fred and Devad narrated as necessary. Sichuan Province was spectacular, and the pictures elicited many questions until they showed pictures of the monastery and began talking about how God had changed their lives and the lives of the monks. When this section began, the group grew quiet, not knowing quite what to say. As the travelers talked of the unusual events – the rainstorm, the chief monk's vision, the language issue, and other events, one by one the group became more interested and once again began asking questions. There were two holdouts: Ellen Smyth, who sat ramrod straight like one possessed, a fitting description of her life, when their spiritual experiences were described – and Kris Gustafson, who tilted back his chair, crossed his arms, and looked down his nose with an expression of skeptical incredulity.

The library was quietly animated, and, for the time being, the cookies and beverages were forgotten. Most of those in the room had been with Lady Ellen Smyth for years. The two most recent arrivals were Kris Gustafson and Devadas himself. During their tenure at The Planes, they had all been forbidden to make any reference to Jesus, God, or the Bible. Their interest paralleled being in a wilderness without food or water for those years. It was as though the advent of Devadas into the household had brought with it a soft, warm breeze, the promise of things to come, a promise that brought hope.

After the account of their adventures and the many miraculous events that accompanied them, Devadas motioned to the group that he had some things that he needed to share with them all, as all had had a role in his upbringing. At this Fred moved back, picked up some more cookies and a cup of mulled cider, and sat down toward the back of the room. He had an inkling that Devad wanted to tell the group what he knew about his life to date, what he had ascertained God had been doing, and how His love had impacted him.

Devadas stood front center. The group wondered what he was about to say, and their total attention was focused on him. Other than Lady Smyth, he addressed them all by their first names.

"Mother, Hannah, Eliza, Mary, Elizabeth, John, James, Jeb, and Fred: I wish to use this opportunity to thank you for loving and caring for me these past fourteen years, and, Kris, for your patience in teaching me."

Then he turned toward his mother, "I can't tell you how much I love you and value you. Mom." With that he used for the first time the informal term of endearment, and he continued, "I love you with a special love. I don't know who my biological mother is, but you are the best mother a boy could have."

At this Ellen Smyth dropped her head, closed her eyes, and began to cry. The cold stiffness of only minutes before melted at the expression of Devadas' love. All her reserve was gone and her acceptance so long ago of the dark side was replaced by something else, something she had never before experienced. She had tasted love, but now it flooded her heart and with it came freedom. The first she had ever known. What she experienced was as unusual and miraculous as Fred's and Devadas' experiences in China – she was sure of it. She lifted her head, lifted it as to someone that no one else see, in an expression of thanks – thanks to God. She glowed, and, had the lights in room been out, her countenance would have lighted the room.

Devadas watched with warm pleasure, relief, and joy and thanked God silently for his mother's new life, but, continuing to hold eye contact with all, said, " Fred shared with me the unusual circumstances of my arrival. I think I know who it was that brought me, and perhaps you sensed that as well. In my opinion he was, he is, the epitome of evil, 'Satan' himself. He obviously had plans for me and was using you to accomplish those intentions. He cares little about who he uses or how he uses people. The dream I had, reinforced my conclusion about this. That I should be so 'honored' to have been selected for his nefarious deeds is truly frightening, but the God of love, the One who sent his only Son, Jesus the Christ, had different plans, plans for good and not for evil, and He has seen fit to bring me into His kingdom, to serve Him, and to preach the Good News to all."

At this he shared the bits and pieces of the puzzle of how God had wooed him, even to the discussions about life, worldview, and truth he had debated with Kris Gustafson.

With that Kris Gustafson noisily slammed his chair down and said with an oath, "Enough of this nonsense. I'm out of here."

He angrily left the room, went to his quarters, packed his things and left The Planes.

When Devadas had finishing sharing his spiritual odyssey, his mother rose, went to the front of the room, and joined him. As she hugged and kissed him resoundingly on the forehead, she said, "Please forgive me, my son, for my part in this horrible plan. I was never taken into his confidence," speaking of Satan, "because he never confides or shares anything with those he uses, but only treats them with the same contempt that he has for God."

Now it was Devadas' turn, and he hugged his mother with the same intensity. As he did so, the tears flowed down his cheeks with joy and forgiveness. "I forgive you, Mom! You were deceived by his duplicity like everyone else."

At this, all the others stood up, applauded, and cheered. When the noise quieted down, John Hodge moved forward and stood by Devadas and his mother.

"Lady Smyth talked with Hannah, Mary and I after Devadas had that terrible dream or vision. I shared with them my anger with God for taking Meg from me after suffering so long with cancer. I was wrong and hateful to feel such bitterness toward God."

At that he bowed his head and cried out, "Lord God! Forgive me, I am so sorry. Cleanse me from my sin, anger and my disbelief."

And the staid John Hodge wept openly and embraced Devadas and Lady Smyth in his joy, relief and enthusiasm. Miracle of miracles, Ellen returned the hug.

The evening had turned into a revival meeting, for one by one each of the others knelt by their chairs and confessed to God that they were sinners in need of His saving love. One, Eliza Bedell, announced that she had once made a decision for Christ, but, before marrying Jeb, had pushed Christ aside and out her life.

Someone said, "I think we should sing a hymn."

Others echoed this idea, and Mary Tompkins began singing, 'Amazing Grace.' Several knew the first verse, a few others knew the last verse, but Mary knew six verses, and taught them to the group.

> Amazing grace! How sweet the sound
> That saved a wretch like me!
> I once was lost, but now am found,
> Was blind but now I see.
> 'Twas grace that taught my heart to fear,
> And grace my fears relieved;
> How precious did that grace appear
> The hour I first believed!
> Through many dangers, toils and snares,
> I have already come;
> 'Tis grace hath brought me safe thus far,
> And grace will lead me home.
> The Lord has promised good to me,
> His word my hope secures;
> He will my shield and portion be
> As long as life endures.
> Yea, when this flesh and heart shall fail,
> And mortal life shall cease,
> I shall posses within the veil,
> A life of joy and peace.
> When we've been there ten thousand years,
> Bright shining as the sun,
> We've no less days to sing God's praise
> Than when we've first begun.

"Where did you learn that old hymn?" asked Ellen Smyth.

Mary responded, "I was part of a campus group called Inter-Varsity Christian Fellowship for a couple of years and often played the piano for their meetings. I was fascinated by the claims of Jesus, but then met the man I eventually married and divorced, and that was the end of it. My choice of a marriage partner, rather than Christ, was wrong from the beginning, and I've so often regretted it."

Fred hadn't said much but had listened intently. Finally, he went to the front of the room and said, "I was almost as skeptical about this religious thing as Kris is, but when you come face to face with situations you are unable to control…." and he grunted for emphasis.

"I've always wanted to be in charge, and I learned on our trip that it just isn't possible. When you come face to face with your own mortality and look into the leering eyes of death, it makes a believer out of you, literally. And, oddly, I have become very close to one who is much more intelligent than I, and who is much more sensitive, someone who can see the hand of God in places and situations," and he shrugged his shoulders, " that I'm blind to. But I want to alert you to something that I learned by experience. We're not out of the woods yet. One of the characteristics Devadas and I have seen in Satan is a fierce and terrible anger. Except for the grace of God that we just sang about, Devadas and I would be dead by now. God has protected us from Satan's fury, and you all have made decisions – except Kris – that have eternal implications. From a human perspective it is frightening what is possibly yet to come."

"Fred's warning is right," added Lady Smyth. "I know, for I have been under his control for most of my life. Satan has only hatred, no compassion. I think what we have heard from Fred's and Devadas' comments is that we all need to pray for God's protection and deliverance.

"The hour is getting late. I don't know what tomorrow will bring, but we need to call it a day, go to our quarters, and get some sleep. Devad, God has used you in all our lives. Would you do a bedtime prayer for us?"

"Yes, Mom, I'd be privileged to do that," responded Devad.

"Holy, kind and gracious God, I don't know what you are about, but I do know that we can trust you completely. Help us to be confident in your watchful care, and protect us from the evil one. I pray this in Jesus' name, Amen!"

With that all gathered the remains of their snacks and carried them to the kitchen. Hodge straightened up the chairs and turned out the lights. The books, maps and all could wait until tomorrow.

Chapter 17
MAKING THE BREAK

Sometime around 2:30 am, Fred was awakened by Taffy's jumping up and down on the bed, frantically barking. Fred hadn't slept so well since he and Devadas left for Asia. As he rubbed his eyes and tried to focus his mind on where he was and who was making all the din, he roused enough to see the flickering of light on the wall of his bedroom. He now was suddenly awake and ran to the window to look out at the Castle.

From Fred's cottage he looked at the backside of the building. On the top floor were rooms where unused items – furniture, kitchen materials, books, and miscellany – were stored. It is also where Leily Borhan had lived when she was Devadas' tutor/teacher. The entire wing of the building was ablaze. Fred pulled on his trousers, slipped into his shoes, and ran to the mansion. As he ran, he wondered why the alarms hadn't gone off. That they hadn't sounded was very odd. His pounding on the back door – it was locked, which also was unusual – finally roused the Bedells whose apartment was near the kitchen.

When Fred shouted what was happening, Eliza hurried out into the hall with her flashlight to awaken everybody, for oddly there were no lights and no electricity. Jeb, in his nightshirt, always the maintenance man, checked the water pressure at the kitchen sink. There was no water - none. He went to the phone to dial 911. The phone was dead. He rushed back in his bedroom to get his cell phone, and there was no signal. It seemed The Planes was cut off from all outside help.

While Eliza was waking those sleeping, Jeb was almost beside himself trying to comprehend why the physical systems of the building were non-functional. In the meantime, Fred had rushed to wake James Simms whose apartment was over the garage. When Simms came to the door, and looked out and saw the flames, he exclaimed, "Oh my God, what is happening?"

It seemed like hours, but in fact it was only minutes before all those living at The Planes were gathered out in the courtyard watching the fire.

Jeb exclaimed, "I don't get it. We have no electricity and no backup, so the gates won't work, and we have no water or phones. Even the cell phones don't work. We can't even call for help."

At that, Simms rushed back into the garage, for he remembered that one of the trucks had a Citizens Band radio.

"Who could possibly be on a CB at this hour of the night or morning," he wondered as he turned it on to channel 9 - which the police used to monitor. There was nothing but static. He adjusted the squelch, but there was still nothing, so he went to channel 19, which is traditionally monitored by truckers when they travel. Wonder of wonders, there was some talk on 19.

"Breaker 19, breaker 19," Simms yelled into the microphone, "can anyone here me? We need help."

With that a voice responded in a decidedly southern accent, "Hey buddy, what's the problem?"

Simms anxiously explained what was happening.

His respondent replied, "I'm out here on the Interstate. Give me your "20," and I will see if I can raise somebody to help."

"What's my "20?" What do you mean by that?" Sims nearly screamed into the microphone.

"Where is the fire located?" responded the trucker.

Sims quickly gave the trucker The Planes' location and shouted, "Hurry."

By now the fire had spread through much of the Castle. The intensity of the fire had grown to the point that the courtyard was no longer a safe place. In addition the wind had begun to blow, and sparks from the fire were being blown over the other buildings. One by one they began burning.

The men hurried to get the cars and equipment out of the garage, but the fire seemed to have a crazed life of its own that prevented doing much more.

James Simms looked on in frustration and despair as the garage burned quickly. They were able only to save the vehicles farthest from the Castle. Simms beloved MG TC was parked in what he had regarded as a safe spot toward the back of the garage, so he sorrowfully had to leave it.

Twice Chosen

The cars and easily-moved equipment were taken down the long drive toward the main gate where Ellen, Devadas, and the staff had already gathered. They were a sorry-looking lot, for the clothes they wore were those they could grab as they hurried from the building.

As they stood, huddled together, the wind was blowing harder, and they noticed the temperature seemed to be dropping.

By now the message about the fire had finally gotten to the authorities, and fire trucks were approaching from both directions. As they pulled up to the gate, Jed called out that there was no power, and the mechanism that worked the gates would not work at all without power.

At this the firemen in the first truck found a large chain in their gear and hooked it securely to the latch end of the gate. While all the other firemen looked on, the largest truck was set in place and the chain was attached from the gate to the truck.

As the truck strained to open the gate, they realized that one truck by itself wasn't enough, so they added another truck to the first. Together, they were finally able to pull the gate from the latch mechanism so the trucks could enter.

By the time the trucks got close to the Castle and other buildings, there was little anyone could do, and the firemen watched helplessly until the fire burnt itself out the next day.

In the meantime the EMS trucks were administering aid to the residents. None were hurt, but all were chilled by exposure and their emotions in watching a significant part of their lives being destroyed before their eyes. Amidst tears of relief and regret, quiet thought and discussion, blankets were handed out, and hot drinks appeared from somewhere. It was evident that since all was lost – papers, identification, credit cards, and all the things that enable people independence – they would need shelter in a safe environment.

One of the EMS drivers attended a church that operated a homeless shelter in Center City called the Prodigal Mission that when called, agreed to provide housing and food for all, including Taffy who was being held in Fred's arms, until details could be sorted out.

Since Jeb and Simms had been able to get three vehicles from the garage before it, too, was engulfed in flames, they would be able to carry everyone and follow the EMS truck down town to the Mission.

Before they split up and went to the cars, Devadas spoke up, "I think we should give God thanks for the fact that we are all alive."

With that all lowered their heads in thanksgiving. John Hodge, without prompting, prayed a prayer they would all remember.

"Lord God! Father in heaven! Tonight you have met us in a most miraculous way. First, you have protected us from being killed by a great inferno. Not one of us had even a hair singed by the blaze. Second, you spared us from the punishment due us by our rebellion. We are saved, not just from the fire that destroyed our home and livelihood for these many years, but we have been saved from the very fires of hell itself. We are eternally grateful for your love, grace and mercy. We give ourselves to you as your humble servants. Amen!"

And with that, all echoed his Amen with their own.

⌒

The Prodigal mission was east of downtown in a very depressed part of the city. There were many boarded up stores, and the ones that appeared to be open during business hours had metal bars over their windows and doors.

Their late arrival was greeted in a manner that suggested that the mission did this all the time – which really seemed unlikely. The director, Eddie Morales, and his wife Yola took the newcomers to their respective wings and found clothes that fit, sort of, for each. All had to be very quiet because the other "guests" were sleeping.

It was early morning, still dark, and the streets were deserted. There was parking in front of the mission, but it didn't seem safe for the cars were expensive, current models, and top of the line. After they had found suitable clothes, James Simms and Fred Riley went out on the street where James asked, "What do you think we ought to do with the cars? This is a pretty seedy part of town."

Fred answered, "I'm not sure. I don't think we should leave them on the street even if it will be daylight in an hour or so. If we do, they may be stolen or stripped. Do you have any money, Simms?"

"Gosh no! Everything was lost in the fire," answered Simms. "Do you?"

"A little and I have my credit cards. Remember – no of course you wouldn't – but when I ran out of the cottage, I slid into my trousers, and, fortunately, my wallet was in the pocket. The reason I asked is there might be a parking area somewhere nearby that is manned. I'd sure feel a lot better about having the cars where somebody is looking after them."

At that moment Jeb walked up saying, "This part of town looks pretty grim. What are we going to do with the cars?"

"We were just talking about that," answered Simms. "I don't think we should leave the cars on the street. Maybe the mission director or somebody else inside can give us some ideas."

"Right," replied Jeb. "I'll find that Morales fellow and ask him. You and Fred stay here and keep an eye on things."

Jeb hurried toward the mission.

Twice Chosen

"This night beats anything I've ever seen," grunted Jeb, talking to himself. "First, Devad and Fred get home after being in Asia, and we had that revival meeting, and then everybody goes to their quarters talking about God's presence, and now everything is gone – or at least most of it. We were living pretty "high on the hog", our digs were the best, and now just a few hours later, we're reduced to living in a mission in the poorest part of town. I know we are lucky to be alive, but, I really don't get it."

༺࿓༻

As Fred and Simms stood on the sidewalk in front of the Mission, Fred rubbed his hand through his blond hair, now grown out since he hadn't been to a barber in weeks, and looked thoughtful.

"When we were on the trip to Tibet and China, Devadas, Lee and I had a lot of time to talk. These events weren't accidental. From my limited grasp of this new life we share, I think we've been participants in a spiritual battle. Devadas' comments and my observations over these past 14 years seem to point to the Evil One. You probably remember when Devadas was brought to the Planes in the cardboard box. Did you see the One that brought him? I didn't, but I've been told about him." At this Fred shuddered at the thought and then went on, "He told Lady Smyth to take the baby and raise him. Why did Lady Smyth agree to do that? And then there was that strange Leily Borhan."

Simms added, "And Kris Gustafson was a bit odd too, in my opinion, but go on with what you were saying."

"Devadas' education was unusual, no doubt about it, and years later Devad had that strange nightmare or vision or whatever it was. It seemed that the boy was being personally trained to be his…," he paused, searching through his mind. "To be his. . ."

"Puppet?" answered Simms.

"That's it. His "puppet" – someone who would do his bidding, someone who could convince the world that he was the savior of mankind. As I understand it, Satan has been trying to strip the creation from God since he was thrown out of heaven. Actually, I don't understand this at all, but the Bible is all about this spiritual battle. Jesus Christ won this battle on the cross. . ."

". . . . but Satan hates all men. The Bible says that man is made in God's own image, so we are God's ultimate creation. Not even the angels can make that claim." And Devadas added his own insight, finishing the sentence, for he had walked up behind them without either of them hearing his approach.

"Hey Devad, I though you were inside helping the ladies," said Simms, nodding toward the neon sign with the cross above it, blinking The Prodigal.

"What do you have there?" asked Fred as he noticed that Devadas was carrying Taffy in his arms. When he reached out to take his dog, Taffy eagerly leapt into his arms and quickly licked his face.

"She looked lonesome, so I decided to come looking for you two guys. Jeb has been talking to the mission director about what to do with the cars. Eddie said that leaving the cars on the street wasn't a good idea, but I didn't hear where he thought they should be parked. They will be out in a few minutes."

Just then Eddie and Jeb walked up.

"Eddie says that we should park the cars in the fenced lot where he keeps his car. They have a man that looks after things during the night, a sort of watchman," said Jeb.

"Buck is almost a permanent resident here at the mission," said Eddie. "It is one of the ways he helps me here. He staggered in here one night, dead drunk and at the end of his rope, but that's another story. Let's get the cars off the street. Jim, you and I will lead the way."

Calling Simms 'Jim' had a ring of familiarity to it that neither Devadas nor Fred was comfortable with. "I think there are going to be a lot more changes than losing The Planes," whispered Devadas to Fred.

"I agree," Fred responded, "you want to ride over with me?"

"I think I should go back and stay with mother," answered Devadas. "I don't know quite what to think about her. She is definitely not herself tonight. She seems more relaxed and free than I've ever seen her. Hey! You better get going. The other guys are waiting for you." Devadas walked quickly back into the Mission.

⁂

The Mission wasn't really one building but rather several buildings, actually four adjacent to one another. At one time each had been a store of some kind, but when the mission was begun, they had been connected and divided into a series of areas – some large and some small.

The main building, and the largest, was a two-story structure. On its front above the door was a large sign in the form of a cross. It was outlined by red neon lights. On the top vertical section, spelled out in green lights, was the word 'THE,' and on lower portion the word 'MISSION.' The horizontal section contained the single word, 'PRODIGAL.'

Entering from the street, the main entrance was a foyer with a floor of wide wooden boards, several benches, and hooks to hang hats and coats.

Further in was a large carpeted area called the Gathering Room where they held services. On the end away from the street was a platform about a foot high, on which there was a podium or lectern, and on the back were several chairs. To the right on the platform was a piano, a keyboard, and a drum set, and on the left, again on the platform, were three crosses, the center one standing taller than the other two. On the back wall behind the crosses was painted what was created in the artist's mind the city of Jerusalem with the temple in the background as it might have appeared from the site of Jesus' crucifixion. There were about sixty chairs, approximately thirty on each side, and a center aisle leading to the platform.

In the areas behind the Gathering Room were a small chapel, counseling rooms, toilets, and a stairway to the second floor where there were quarters for staff, and guests.

Adjacent to the Gathering Room just described and on the right while facing the building from the street was the women's dorm with bunks, lockers, very nice bath facilities, a spacious dressing room, and a comfortable lounge for informal visiting. The women's area was tastefully done with pictures and other decorative touches.

There were two areas (buildings) to the left of the Gathering Room. The first held the dining room, not at all like an institution, but friendly and inviting with tablecloths and comfortable chairs. Behind the dining room was a well-equipped kitchen with a large pantry, walk-in cooler, and freezer.

The building beyond the dining room/kitchen area was the men's dormitory which was much like the women's on the opposite end of the mission, but done in a masculine motif and without the dressing room.

All units were connected to one another with the main entrance being that into the Gathering Room. The kitchen had access to the alley behind the mission for deliveries, and there were emergency exits that opened from the inside while sounding an alarm.

When Devadas went back into the mission, only John Hodge was in the Gathering Room, and he was reading a Bible he had picked up from one of the folding chairs. He looked worn-out, and the light from the overhead fluorescent lights seemed to make him appear almost ashen. This night had been especially hard on him. He was, after all, in his late seventy's. He looked up when he heard Devad enter.

"Hodge – or should I call you Mr. Hodge – are you all right? You don't look too well," asked Devadas.

"Truthfully, I don't feel well either. I'm totally worn out. I decided to stay up for a while to make sure you find where you will sleep. It has been a most dreadful, no, that's not right; it has been a most "eventful" day. I'm so blessed to get to know Meg's Jesus. Now, regardless of what happens to me, I will be reunited with my beloved wife."

At this Devadas felt his eyes well up with tears. He had grown to love John Hodge, so he sat down beside him and asked if he could pray.

John Hodge smiled weakly and bowed his head.

Devadas prayed, "Lord Jesus, thank you for bringing my brother John into you kingdom. Thank you for your forgiveness and limitless love. Fill John with your presence and strength, and help him sleep well tonight, the rest that comes from the peace of knowing You. Thank You for Your protection in the past, now, and through all eternity. In Your wonderful, precious and Holy Name, Amen!"

John returned the Bible to the chair beside him and stood up, as did Devadas, and the two embraced – a boy and the grandfather he never knew. "Come, my boy. You are to sleep upstairs, as am I. We will share a room. The beds are ready. We have so much to be thankful for," and he turned toward the stairs with Devadas right behind him.

It was only a short time later that Fred, Jeb and James Simms returned with Eddie Morales after parking the cars.

"Thanks for sharing the story about the Smyth mansion and Devadas. We'll have to get Devadas to share his story with our guests. That will grab their attention for sure."

"Jeb, your wife is upstairs in room 3." He pointed toward the men's end. "Jim and Fred will sleep in the men's dorm. We have enough beds. You have looked in there? Just pick an empty bunk. All the bedding is clean. If you need more blankets, they are on a shelf near the bathroom door. I'm going upstairs to my apartment. My wife will think something happened to me."

The men turned and walked across the dining room to the men's dorm.

"Thanks for everything!" Simms said softly, "I'm ready to hit the hay."

'I'll say!" Fred agreed, "See you in the morning, if we can wake up."

As Jeb and Eddie softly climbed the stairs, Eddie's voice carried to them, "Sleep well. God is so-o-o good."

And he could be heard humming what sounded like a hymn as he continued to his apartment and Jeb went on to join Eliza in their room.

Chapter 18

A Glorious Encounter

Ellen Smyth had never felt more freedom then when she threw herself on God's mercy and accepted the saving work of Jesus Christ. Ever since she had made the terrible mistake of bargaining with the "Prince of this World," she had been miserable. She had never loved Edgar, poor man. Her deceased husband and supposed rescuer promised to be her path to excitement, prominence and wealth, but, in her ignorance and desperation, she had compromised what she instinctively knew was right and made the deal that led to her bondage and the control of her every thought and action.

When Devadas was brought to The Planes that afternoon some fourteen years before, the Evil One to whom Ellen Smyth considered herself obligated believed that he had the perfect plan by which he could achieve his goal of thwarting God. The boy would be raised in a privileged environment, devoid of love, where cost would be no barrier and carefully selected teachers could shape the boy's perspective into selfish ambition, and his charm could be polished to a brilliance that could captivate people and nations in the battle for men's souls.

In Genesis 50:20, Joseph, when addressing his brothers, said, "You intended to harm me, but God intended it for good." (NIV)

Satan had evil plans for Devadas, Ellen Smyth, and the entire household of The Planes, but God intended it all for good – and so it was.

The moment the boy was brought to the estate, things changed. First, the household had compassion on the child and treated him with love and tender care. Later, Ellen Smyth's heart was warmed by his presence, and her icy spirit began to melt. Love replaced indifference and hostility, and that love began to express itself in myriad ways.

The culmination of change occurred with the return of Devadas and Fred from China. There was a spirit about them, an aura of something heavenly. Their testimonies were energized by the Spirit of God, and Ellen Smyth and her entire household were saved – saved *from* themselves and *to* the Almighty God. There was great rejoicing in The Planes and great rejoicing in heaven as well, had they be able to see it.

Yet, there was unfinished business. Satan and his followers were insanely angered by these events and vowed retribution. Since God's divine protection covered his newly born children, Satan's anger was directed to what he could destroy – and he did it with a vengeance. Fire, an unholy fire, seemed to have burnt even the brick and rock of the place that had been the focus of his nefarious intent.

Even though late, sleep escaped Ellen Smyth as she lay on her bed. These were the thoughts that raced this way and that through her mind. She was not anxious, at least not in a negative way, but was anticipating the future – a future that included her adopted son, and her heavenly Father. She could hardly wait to see what would happen next.

And she finally went to sleep as her heart smiled within her.

As she slept, she saw herself walking in a garden. All around her were trees, shrubs, and flowers of all kinds, and the scents of these flowers were mixed with the scent of distant rain. Then there were the sounds: the melodious sounds of singing birds, a breeze gently moving through the trees, and, in the distance, the burbling of a brook. She was following a path of some kind, and as she walked she came to a bench by the brook she had heard. She sat down, absorbing the beauty all around her.

As she sat, totally at peace, she realized that another was sitting beside her. She turned to look at her companion and knew instinctively that it was Jesus. They sat together, neither talking, and the peace and contentment of this encounter would linger in her mind forever.

After a time Jesus looked into her face with great love and, speaking tenderly, said. "My daughter, you must no longer call the boy Devadas, a name I despise, but call him David, for he is my beloved child."

At that she awoke. She swung her feet to the side of the bed, and sat up wide-awake.

"I have seen Jesus. I have been with my Lord. He has spoken to me, his servant."

And she slid off the bed to kneel, and, raising her arms, praised God.

Chapter 19

A New Day!

Morning comes early at The Prodigal. The unwritten rule of the mission was: "The idle mind is the devil's workshop," or the verses in Proverbs 6:6-11:

> "Go to the ant, you sluggard;
> Consider its ways and be wise
> It has no commander,
> No overseer or ruler,
> Yet it stores its provisions in summer
> And gathers its food at harvest
> How long will you lie there, you sluggard?
> When will you get up from your sleep?
> A little sleep, a little slumber,
> A little folding of the hands to rest -
> And poverty will come on you like a bandit
> And scarcity like an armed man."

Inside both dorms everybody was ready for breakfast, which was served promptly at 7 am. Fred Riley and James Simms had only a couple hours of sleep, while the ladies, Elizabeth Wood, Hannah Desmaris and Mary Tompkins, had fared a bit better, but none were prepared for the flurry of activity that surrounded them.

In both dorms there was one semi-permanent guest who was assigned the responsibility of each respective area. These individuals made sure newcomers learned the 'what and when' of things needing to be done: the sequencing of showers, where to keep clothes, how to make the bunks, cleaning responsibilities etc. Simms said it was like being in the army.

The man assigned on the men's end went by the name Ashe. He never said whether that was a name or a nickname. He was pretty private about himself, but he was a helpful and affable fellow. He got the guys in and out of the shower sequence in jig time and showed them where the brooms and other cleaning supplies were kept so they could do their chores after breakfast.

The men's dorm was nearly full. Actually, there were only one or two beds that weren't slept in. Ashe said this was typical, but when the weather got really cold they would sometimes have to set up cots in the Gathering Room.

It was different for the ladies. Their dorm supervisor was a youngish woman called Doris. She wasn't very big, but she was tough and spared no quarter. Mary, the sensitive musician was quite taken aback, but dutifully did as she was told. Neither Hannah nor Elizabeth seemed fazed by her abrupt manner.

The women's dorm was only about half-full. The women were friendly enough but kept to themselves. Two were really young girls who appeared to be about fourteen or fifteen years old. Most of the time they lived on the streets, selling themselves to support their drug habits. Both were stick thin and wasted appearing. Hannah was immediately taken to them and tried to engage them in conversation, but they were very private, and as soon as they had eaten a little breakfast and done their chores, disappeared back into the city. Doris shook her head their direction as they went out.

"Those two are pretty hard case."

Everyone ate at the same time, and today one of the cooks offered thanks. The food was quite tasty. The coffee would float an anchor but was fresh, hot and good. Other than juice, toast and day old rolls (donated by a local bakery), oatmeal, sausage, poached eggs with hard yolks, and grits filled out the menu. Nothing was up to Eliza's standards, but if anyone left the table hungry, it was his or her own fault.

The staff from The Planes ate at the same long table. Before they began bussing the dishes, Ellen Smyth got their attention.

"After we do our morning chores, we need to discuss what we do next. Does anyone have a suggestion where we might meet that would be quiet, and wouldn't have any interruptions?"

Yola Morales overheard Ellen's question and came over to their table.

"You could use the chapel. We don't use it until 10 am. If you can be done by then, it should be about perfect."

Twice Chosen

"Thank you!" Then turning back to her table continued. "That is what we will do. We will meet in the chapel right after the dish and cleaning crews are done."

Then it occurred to Ellen to ask Yola, "How long does it usually take for the jobs to be done?"

"They should all be done by 9 am."

And Yola went back to join her husband as they too, were clearing their table.

Devadas had been assigned to help wash dishes in the kitchen. His helper was Ashe. Their responsibility was to load the dish racks and keep the dishwasher going. He and Devadas bonded immediately.

"How long have you been here?" asked Devadas.

"Almost fifteen years."

"You came here about the time I was born!"

"You're fourteen then?"

"What brought you here?"

Devadas wasn't sure whether Ashe would reply, for there was a long silence.

"They found me dead drunk in the alley behind the mission."

"Who found you?"

"One of the guys doing breakfast in the kitchen. He went and got Charlie Hamn, and, together, they dragged me in and threw me in the shower. I think I must have smelled pretty bad."

"So who was Charlie Hamn?"

"He was director before Eddie. Nice guy, Charlie."

"So what did they do to you?" continued Devadas.

"They tore the clothes off me and scrubbed me with soap and a brush like that one over there where Max is washing pots and pans. By the time they was finished, I was comin' to. They about rubbed my skin clean off."

"And then what?"

"I was swearin' at everybody, and they dragged me out and threw me a towel." 'Git yourself dried off,' Charlie demanded. Then they got me some clean clothes. By the time I was dressed, I was calming down. After a couple cups of coffee – and the coffee then was just as strong as it is now – they escorted me to a bunk to let me sleep off the rest of my drunk. They had to clean me up a couple of times 'cause I puked all over everything. I always said it probably was the coffee."

Devadas looked at his watch. It was almost 9 am.

"I want to hear the rest of your story - later. I must go. We have a meeting in the chapel."

Ashe grunted as Devadas threw his apron in the hamper and raced from the room.

Devadas was the last one to enter. As he came in all applauded. He did a little bow, grinned, and responded, "Thank you, thank you, one and all."

And he sat down. As he did, he noticed his mother looking at him in an odd sort of way, as if seeing him for the first time.

Ellen Smyth moved to the front of the room and stood behind the pulpit, put down her notebook, adjusted her glasses, and began.

"Thank you for all being here promptly. We have a lot to discuss. First, I hate to do this but I'm afraid I must, you are all dismissed from your responsibilities at The Planes."

At this pronouncement all in the room expressed sounds of denial and disbelief.

Devadas stood up and said - leaning forward with his hands on the pew in front of him, "Mom! You can't! These are not just employees but our friends. We can't dismiss them. What will they do, where will they go?"

"I have talked to both my lawyer and accountant. This is the way things stand at this time. Let me explain."

"From all reports, The Planes was completely destroyed: the Castle, as you often called it, the workshops, garages, barns, green houses; everything. Nothing was saved. I don't understand it. I had been assured that the fire protection systems were first class, and if a fire ever began it would be quickly extinguished with perhaps only some smoke damage being sustained. Mysteriously, all systems failed last night, every one of them. From what I gather after talking to the authorities, there is no evidence of foul play. I was suspicious that Kris Gustafson might have been involved, for his departure last night was at best peculiar. But I really doubt that he did. He was not vindictive. He called me after tracking us down, and was as astonished as we were. Kris is an atheist and thinks Christians are fools. He said that he was simply disgusted by Devadas' and Fred's witness and our decisions."

"Forgive me! I'm getting sidetracked. There are so many bits and pieces of this situation, I seem to go first one way and then another, but back to the dismissal. I have also been informed that during the last twenty-four hours, my assets have all but disappeared. I have a small amount of personal money that I had laid aside, but as far as I know, that is all. I have no money to buy a new home, large or small, and certainly no resources to pay any of you for services rendered. To put it simply, I too am going to have to find a job and a place to live."

"I'm nearly seventy years old. I have never worked except as a barmaid which is what I doing when I met and married Edgar. I have no formal education or experience. To put it bluntly, I am - we are all completely dependent upon God. Basically our assets consist of the three cars that we drove here to the mission. They will have to be sold."

At that moment there was a knock at the chapel door.

Eddie entered and excitedly said, "I have more bad news. The lot where we left the cars so they would be safe was broken into early this morning. My night watchman was caught off guard, knocked unconscious, and your cars were destroyed. I don't understand this at all. All the other vehicles were untouched. I'm so sorry. I was sure they would be safe there. This is my fault."

Devadas brushed his remorse aside. "How is the fellow that minded the lot?"

"He's O.K., but he has a nasty knot on the back of his head. The police were summoned as soon as he came to, but they have no idea who was responsible. They shrugged their shoulders and said it was probably some gang."

Attention turned again to Ellen Smyth, and James Simms asked, "You do have insurance don't you?"

At this Ellen looked at the floor and shook her head no.

"This is another mysterious part of the story. My accountant can find no records for insurance of any kind though he is sure that all premiums were up to date."

Eddie Morales, who was still in the room, commented, "This begins to sound more and more like what happened to Job, though with a few twists. That fire was one thing, the cars are another, and now you are telling all of us that you have no insurance?"

Ellen nodded a yes to this last question, looked him in the eye, and smiling said, "And I've never been happier and more content in my life. Believe it!"

All the others in the room applauded and cheered. Devadas had a huge grin on his face and spoke out, "Remember when Jesus quoted Isaiah and spoke these words:

'The Spirit of the Lord is on me,
because he has anointed me
to preach good news to the poor.
He has sent me to proclaim freedom for the prisoners
And recovery of sight for the blind,
To release the oppressed,
To proclaim the year of the Lord's favor.'" (NIV)

"Sure!" replied the director. "That passage is from Luke, Chapter 4. That was just before his audience tried to push him off a cliff."

"Well, that is what has happened to my mother. Jesus has just freed her from very real and incredible bondage. In fact, you'll never believe this, but this prophecy is true for each of us in this room."

This time the group exploded in applause and cheers.

Eddie sat down. "This I've got to hear. I heard about Devadas last night. Now I need the whole story."

Fred interjected, "There isn't nearly enough time. You said we needed to be done by 10 am."

"But there is one more thing I must say. I have to tell you about my dream last night," interrupted Ellen Smyth.

The chapel became quiet, and all eyes turned toward her.

"In my dream I was walking in a most beautiful garden. I'm quite sure it was in heaven. When the path I was on passed close by a bubbling brook, there was a bench, and I sat down. I wasn't tired. I don't know why I sat down. Then I realized that someone was sitting beside me, and I turned toward where he was. It was Jesus.

"He pronounced, 'You are to change your son's name to David for I detest the name Devadas,' and then I awakened." and she walked over to where Devadas was sitting, took his hand and drew him to her side. "I looked up both names on Eddie's computer this morning. Devadas means 'slave of the gods.' This was the name the Evil One instructed me to use, and indeed that was his plan. But David means 'beloved of God'."

"I wish now to introduce all of you to David – David Lee Smyth. I chose the middle name Lee because it was through David's Lisu friend Lee that he accepted our gracious and loving Lord and Savior, Jesus, our Messiah."

At this there was such a commotion that Yola and a number of other staff members crowded into the chapel to see what was going on. All of Ellen Smyth's ex-staff were giving David and Ellen hugs and high-fives. It was bedlam of the finest sort.

They had to vacate the chapel by 10 am. As Ellen's ex-employees filed from the room, the euphoria of God at work faded, and doubts and questions arose. What were they going to do now? The Planes had been their life.

Elizabeth Wood, Hannah Desmaris, and Mary Tompkins went to the lounge in the women's dorm, so they could talk. They were quite close, for not only had they been co-workers over the years, they were the best of friends.

Elizabeth in her mid-seventies was the first to speak. "I'm going to retire. I have been able to invest a significant portion of my income, so along with social security, from a financial standpoint will be just fine. I want to

Twice Chosen

keep busy. Retirement - at least for now is not for me. How about you, Hannah?"

Hannah in her early 40's, was very industrious, and upbeat.

"You know, truthfully, I'm not at all concerned. I have lots of options. I could find another maid job somewhere or work as a waitress, but I've always wanted to go to school and study law of all things so maybe I'll try that. I see all this in many ways as a great opportunity. What about you, Mary?"

"I haven't a clue. I guess I always assumed that I would work for Lady Smyth until the day I died. I suppose I could teach piano lessons, but I doubt that teaching lessons would either be enough to keep me busy or provide income until retirement. I have some investments, but I don't want to start them yet. I really don't know what I'll do."

Elizabeth suddenly straightened and looked directly into Mary's eyes, "Why don't we get an apartment together. It would help me because I don't have any family. All my siblings are dead. I think it would help you too, Mary; sharing rent and food costs would be a whole lot better than going it alone. If you want to teach piano, we could probably find an apartment – or maybe even buy a house together. I love having you play. And," she added, "we've always been close."

Hannah clapped her hands in approval. "That's a great idea. That would be a perfect solution for both of you. And then I can come and visit, and we can do things together. Great! I wish I thought of it myself." She actually glowed with enthusiasm at the idea.

"Then it's settled," said Elizabeth.

"When do we start?" asked Mary. "Come on girls, let's find a newspaper and the three of us can start studying the want ads."

And all three went to Eddie's office to see if he might have a copy of the day's paper.

While the ladies were excitedly planning their future together, James Simms and Fred Riley had gone to the dining room to get a cup of coffee.

James was leaning back in his chair. "I'm not too concerned about the future, are you?"

Fred was leaning on the table with his right arm supporting his chin and doing circular motions with his cup. Taffy, his cocker spaniel was at his feet. "Not really, well, only a little," he said thoughtfully. "I'm quite sure I can find something. I may not get to do my first love, like at The Planes. I love having my hands in the dirt, but God is in charge of everything.

He paused a moment in remembrance. "I sure enjoyed the time in China at that monastery. I know that was a God-directed moment, and I share Devadas – excuse me – David's enthusiasm for sharing the gospel. . . .

, and I'm pretty ignorant about the Bible, maybe I should go to Bible school or seminary somewhere and get some serious training."

"You'd be a good missionary, I think. You have an easy way with people. Maybe you could connect your interest in botany with missionary work?"

"Who knows! That's a good idea. All this is so new, less than 24 hours, and the reality of not being at The Planes hasn't really hit me."

"And I agree. I really love being around cars. I might even try to set up my own shop. I don't think I'd like to sell cars. Maybe I could get a job as part of a pit crew at Talladega, Darlington, or Daytona. I know some guys. . . ., but I don't know, Sundays are really big in NASCAR. The MG was insured, so that will help with the finances until I find something, and I'm not likely to ever find a replacement."

"Yeah, doing the NASCAR thing would be tough. I've heard about mechanics traveling to the vehicles rather than setting up shop in a fixed location. Really though, I don't have a clue what to advise about that one. It will take a while to get the settlement on the MG."

Fred drained the last few drops from his cup, carried it to the dish window, and put it in the bin with the other dirty cups and spoons.

As he walked back to the table where Simms was sitting, he commented, "I wonder what Jeb and Eliza will do? They've got to be in their late seventies. You'd think they'd retire."

"Retire? Come on Fred - you know better then that. They're both in good health, and that Eliza is a ball of fire. I don't think she ever sits down."

"You got that right, and sometimes I think that Jeb is too ornery to die, though his bark is worse than his bite."

"Well, I think I'll go in and see if they say anything on the TV about the big fire," added Simms, as he too set his coffee cup in the bin in the dish window.

"I'll follow along. I have nothing to do. Besides, lunch won't be ready for an hour and a half." And Fred, with Taffy close behind, followed Simms to where the TV was located.

༄

Promptly at 7 pm, those who wished to have shelter for the night were required to attend a worship service in the Gathering Room. The Prodigal Mission had regular attendees, and many came night after night as long as the weather was cool or cold, but on warmer nights they would avoid the mission, preferring not to have to 'go to church.'

Since the weather was on the cool side and getting colder, a good crowd could be expected. Eddie Morales, always on the lookout for new talent and faces, decided to make the most of his unusual guests. After talking to Ellen

Twice Chosen

Smyth, he decided to go all out. Tonight he would have Mary Tompkins play the piano for the hymn sing, which usually consisted of the staff doing the singing though there were a few of the "guests" who enjoyed the music immensely and would join in with gusto.

Ellen told him that David played the piano nearly as well as Mary, so it was decided that David would play. Then as the high point of the evening, Fred would give his testimony, and David would share whatever God had given him.

It was usually Eddie himself who led the service and did the speaking, but sometimes it would be Yola, or one of the other staff, so this evening's program might just get the attention of some of the regulars who were there only so they could get a night's sleep in a warm clean bed. Eddie had no idea what lay ahead.

∽

The Gathering Place was full. Somehow the word had gotten out that 'those people who were burned out of that big, walled-in estate' were going to do the service, and that brought the curious, cynical and critical in to watch the show. The mission felt more like a P.T. Barnum big top then God's place for the homeless, helpless, and hurting.

The Planes' people were not taking any of this for granted. They spent several hours in prayer and preparation for the evening's service, but none had any expectations because nearly all were new to the church idea. Furthermore, not one had ever been near a mission before, let alone participate in the activities. With a few exceptions only what had been seen on TV gave them any idea of what they could expect.

What would a religious service look like when designed by redeemed renegades of ungodliness? Eddie and Yola Morales and their staff were about to find out. First, prayer wasn't done as an act necessary to sanctify proceedings. Second, music was to uplift the soul and not to promote a musical mantra designed to mesmerize the mind. Third, words spoken were the simple reality of changed lives. Fourth, the Bible was presented as God's word for life. And fifth, the expectation held that the God who had set them free would do the same for the audience. Their faith was a tangible, touchable truth.

Director Morales opened the meeting with prayer.

"Gracious, and wonderful God, thank you for our new friends – new brothers and sisters in Christ. We are blessed by their presence with us. Despite the circumstances of their arrival, we praise you for sending them here. We now give you this service to lead all those involved in whatever manner you choose."

All those from The Planes were introduced with Ellen Smyth being last. As she took the microphone, she stepped down from the platform in order to be nearer the audience. Most of the 'guests,' were off the street and were dirty and disheveled. The smells of alcohol and marijuana mixed with that of body odors were most unsettling. As Ellen moved closer, the unpleasantness brought memories of her childhood flooding her with wave after wave of nausea. She struggled to hold her composure.

"Men and women, I'm glad that you have come tonight. Being with you has reminded me of my childhood in Liverpool, England. My youth was spent in an area a lot like this part of the city. I wanted so badly to escape my circumstances that I became involved with the occult and literally made a pact with the devil – that if he would give me wealth and status, I would be his."

"I married Edgar, a very wealthy American, and moved to this country. Edgar died of cancer, and his wealth and position were mine. Money was my god, and I daily bowed at its altar. In all the glitter of possessions, I had all that money could buy. My every whim was met. I had everything except happiness, contentment, joy and peace."

"You all know the estate that burned last night, so you know what I possessed. But God has intervened, and though I now have nothing, in truth have everything I really wanted. My worldly possessions are gone. They have been replaced by love. God has brought me love. His love came to me first in my beloved son David, and just last night, before the fire, it came to me in Jesus Christ. I am now blessed by the one thing that money cannot buy. I am loved, and whether I live or die, I know that I am loved and will forever more be loved.

"Choose wisely! Love is the most valuable asset. God is the source of love, and He expressed it in sending His own Son, Jesus to die for me – for all of us. He rose again and lives. He lives in me. He has given me life – real life, a life of love. He will do it for you if you will allow it.

"My son, my only son, the one given to me by God, is now going to play the piano for you. In a few minutes he will speak to you. Listen carefully!"

The mission's piano was an old upright. It probably was 100 years old or more. Every night it was used in the evening programs. And, because the streets of the city were filled with the lost and lonely from every walk of life, from time to time one would walk in, and the heart of the old instrument would sing for a few moments in the gnarled and dirty hands of that lost soul.

Tonight, David sat at the keyboard and stroked the keys with an intense love for his Lord. The piano responded in a miraculous and heavenly manner. The sounds that filled the room were the voices of angels singing, "Glory to

God!" David played Bach, Gershwin, Mahler, and Brahms. Time seemed to stand still. The room was still and quiet with awe for the Creator God.

When David finished playing, there was no applause. There was only stunned silence. David took the microphone and did as his mother had done, stepped off the platform to be nearer his audience. The presence of the Holy Spirit was palpable, and the connection was made between the truth - the word of God, and all those present. David's message was simple. It was direct. It was to the point.

"My brothers and sisters. You know that you have run from God. When He has come near you, you have hidden in the shadows. When He has spoken to you, you have shut your ears. When you have been cared for, you have refused to give thanks. You have abandoned your families. You have abandoned your friends. You have rejected every offer of love. You have sought solace in a bottle, a joint or a fix. All these have failed you. You only consider your own counsel, and you are the victims of those lies. Look at yourselves – no, not your clothing, not your companions. No, look at yourselves. You are on the slippery slope to hell. Is life better for you now than before? Each day you are older. Is life easier today than yesterday? You know it isn't. And the worst is yet to come. Now you have the mission for a warm bed and meal. What happens when your drink or drugs are gone? What happens when reality hits?

" God says, 'For all have sinned and come short of the glory of God.' That means that you have missed the mark. The gulf between you and God is far too great to cross. God loves you so much that He gave His one and only son for you, and whoever believes in Him will not perish, will not continue sliding down that slippery slope toward the fiery pit of everlasting punishment, will not experience anguish, thirst, hunger and separation from God; but have everlasting life.

"Do you know what life is? Do you find anything of value in your lives? Jesus said to the Samaritan woman getting water at the well, 'Everyone who drinks this water will be thirsty again, but whoever drinks the water I give him will never thirst. In fact, the water I give him will become in him a spring of water welling up to eternal life.'

"Do you think that death will solve your problems? Some of you are considering that right now. Death doesn't mean nothingness. Death without Jesus only up-ends that slippery slope and down you go into the pit of hell. In Hell you won't have your friends, you'll be forever alone - in torment. Choose life. Choose Christ. Live! The choice is yours. Make it right this time. Let Jesus save you.

"We need to pray.

Lord God, help these men and women to choose Jesus, to choose life. They need your love. They need your peace. They need you. Amen!"

As David said "Amen," there arose a wail of anguish. Men and women fell to their knees, confessed their sin and accepted that wonderful grace of our living Lord. All, including Eddie, Yola, and the staff, fell to their knees. The Spirit moved among the crowd like at Pentecost. Men and women were being saved. Men and women were being revived. Men and women were yielding their lives to the One and Only God.

Epilogue

It was morning, and David had awakened early. He slipped quietly from his bed, put on his clothes and jacket, and went downstairs to take a walk. He didn't think about the dangers of the neighborhood, or even where he was going. He only felt the need to go out and walk.

Alarms were set if exit doors were opened during the night, so David went through the dining room and kitchen because he knew the staff would have the door leading into the alley unlocked. The smell of fresh coffee made him smile, and it was evident that something really good was in the ovens. It almost smelled like the kitchen at The Planes. And then he knew why. Standing at the big stainless steel worktable was Eliza Bedell with her apron on, humming softly. She just couldn't stay away from what she was created to do.

As David walked through, Eliza looked up and smiled.

"Good morning David. You are up bright and early. Isn't it a wonderful morning."

David grinned happily.

"Hi Eliza. God bless you this fine morning. The mission needs you."

"Indeed they do! I told Jeb that they need us. There are lots of things that he can do, and I love being in the kitchen."

As David let himself out the door into the alley, he walked along listening to the sounds of morning and prayed silently in his heart, thanking God for using him last night.

As he walked along, looking at the backs of the building lining the alley, he soon found himself in a residential area – if it could really be called that. Still, people did live there. As he walked, he prayed. These people needed Jesus, and he prayed more intently.

He heard the cry of a baby coming from somewhere.

"Oh Lord God, that child needs you," and he felt tears well up in his young eyes. It all looked somehow familiar to him. Déjà vu? Perhaps!

Ahead was a cardboard carton lying near some garbage cans, one of which was tipped over, lying on its side. He walked to the carton, looked inside, and saw that it was empty. At that he flattened it, set it along the garbage cans, and walked on, praising God and praying for his city.